tiny titans

AW YEAH TITANS!

Art Baltazar & Franco
writers

Art Baltazar
artist & letterer

TINY TITANS: AW YEAH TITANS!

Published by DC Comics. Compilation Copyright © 2013 DC Comics.
All Rights Reserved.

Originally published by DC Comics in single magazine form in
TINY TITANS 45-50 Copyright © 2011, 2012 DC Comics. All Rights
Reserved. All characters, their distinctive likenesses and related
elements featured in this publication are trademarks of DC Comics.
The stories, characters and incidents featured in this publication are
entirely fictional. DC Comics does not read or accept unsolicited
ideas, stories or artwork.

DC Comics, 2900 W. Alameda Avenue, Burbank, CA 91505
Printed by Transcontinental Interglobe Beauceville, QC, Canada.
6/23/16. Third Printing.
ISBN: 978-1-4012-3812-4

PEFC Certified
Printed on paper from
sustainably managed
forests and controlled
sources
PEFC/01-31-106   www.pefc.org

Library of Congress Cataloging-in-Publication Data

Baltazar, Art.
  Aw yeah Titans! / Art Baltazar ; Franco.
    pages cm. -- (Tiny Titans ; volume 8)
    ISBN 978-1-4012-3812-4 (pbk.)
1. Graphic novels. I. Aureliani, Franco, illustrator. II. Title.
PZ7.7.B33Aw 2013
741.5'973–dc23
                              2012048789

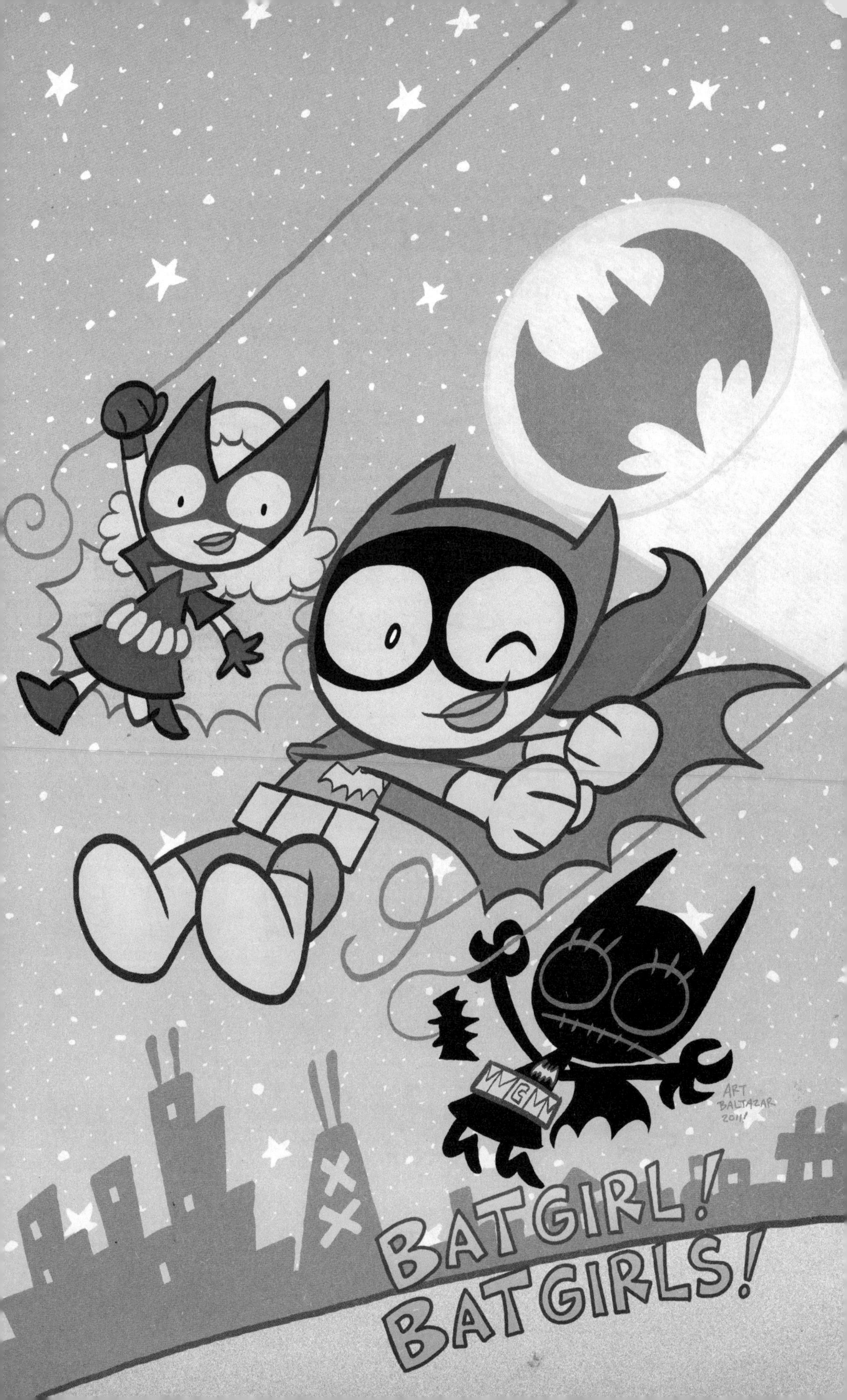

BATGIRL!
BATGIRLS!
ART BALTAZAR 2011!

tiny titans

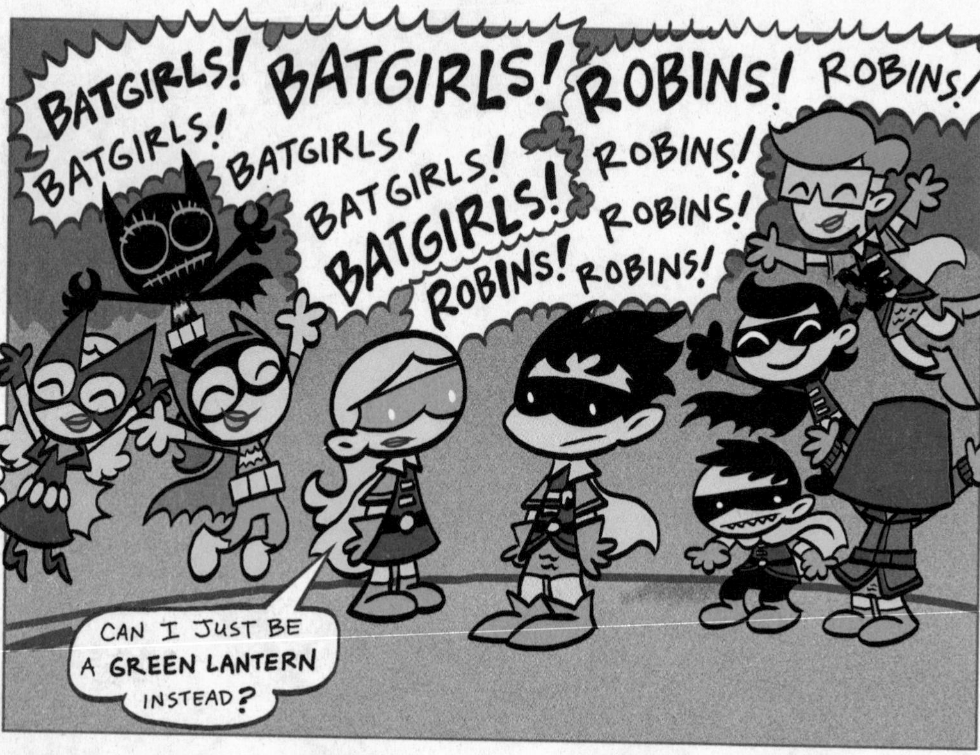
BATGIRLS! BATGIRLS! BATGIRLS! BATGIRLS! BATGIRLS! BATGIRLS!
ROBINS! ROBINS! ROBINS! ROBINS! ROBINS! ROBINS!
CAN I JUST BE A GREEN LANTERN INSTEAD?

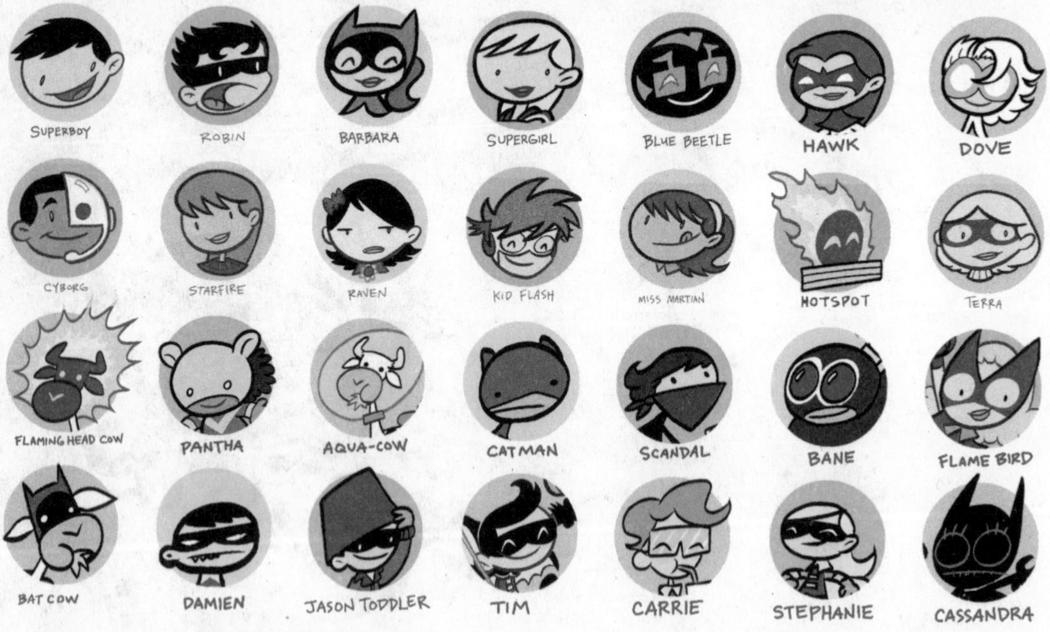
SUPERBOY
ROBIN
BARBARA
SUPERGIRL
BLUE BEETLE
HAWK
DOVE
CYBORG
STARFIRE
RAVEN
KID FLASH
MISS MARTIAN
HOTSPOT
TERRA
FLAMING HEAD COW
PANTHA
AQUA-COW
CATMAN
SCANDAL
BANE
FLAME BIRD
BAT COW
DAMIEN
JASON TODDLER
TIM
CARRIE
STEPHANIE
CASSANDRA

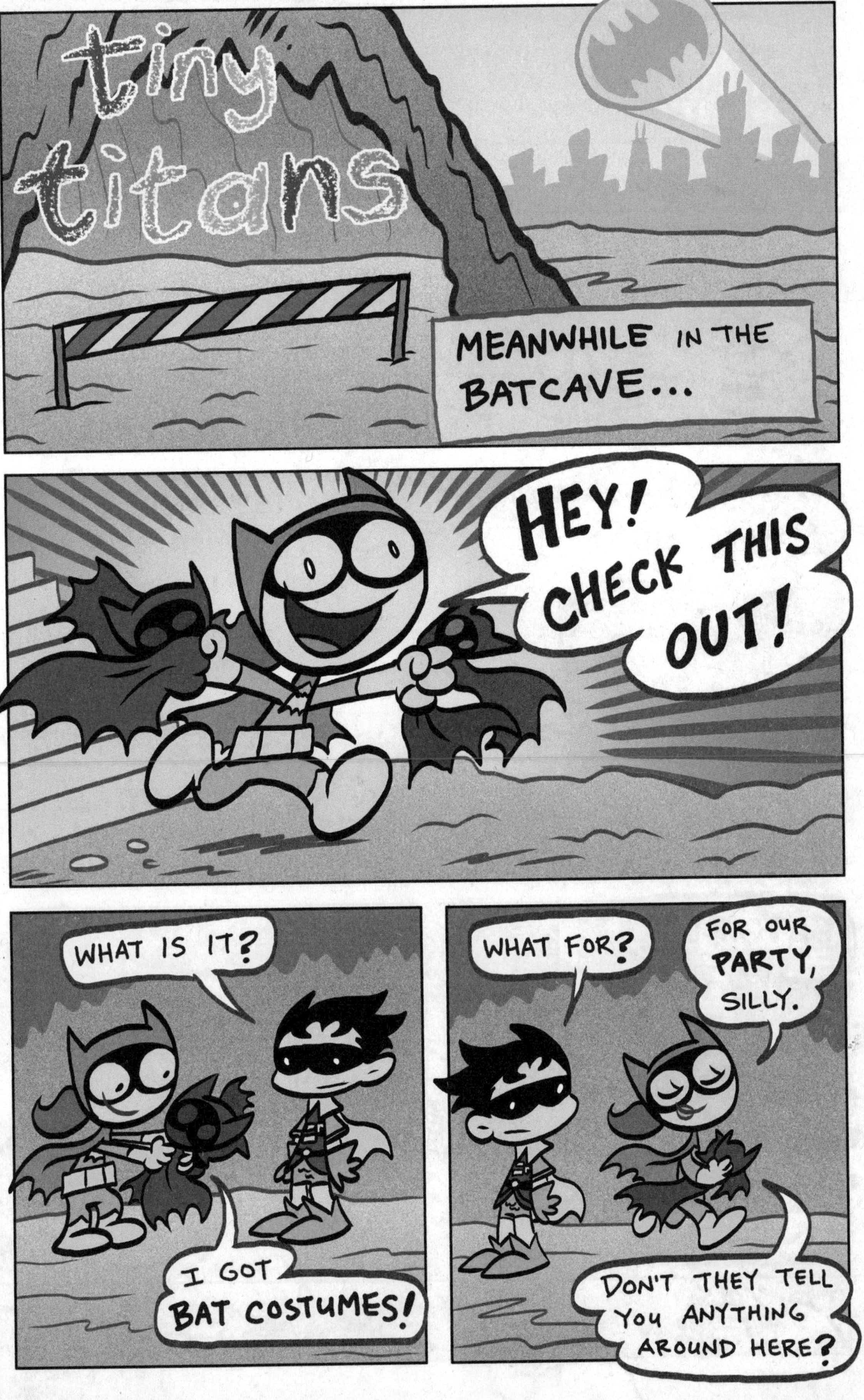
tiny titans
MEANWHILE IN THE BATCAVE...
HEY! CHECK THIS OUT!
WHAT IS IT?
I GOT BAT COSTUMES!
WHAT FOR?
FOR OUR PARTY, SILLY.
DON'T THEY TELL YOU ANYTHING AROUND HERE?

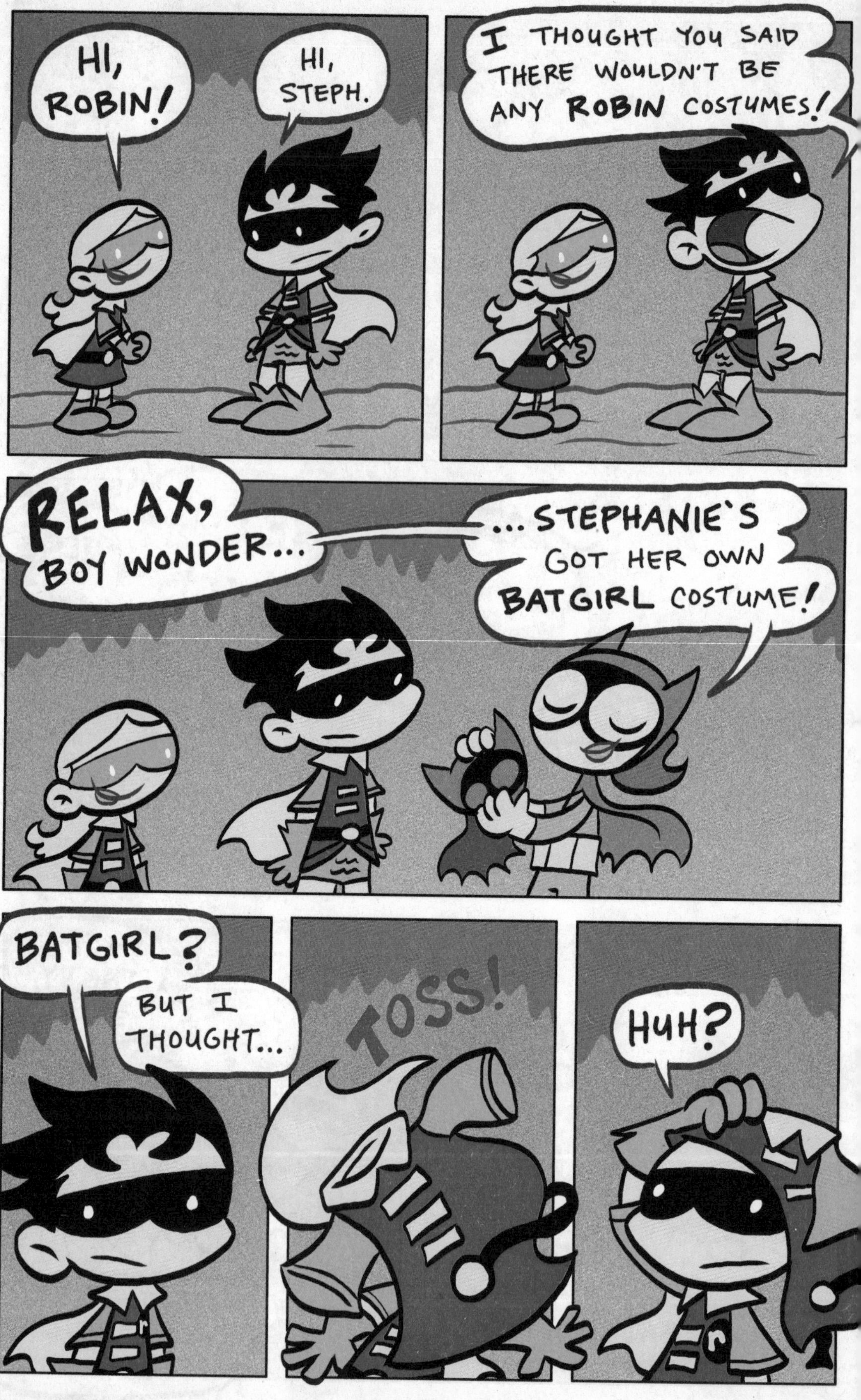
HI, ROBIN!
HI, STEPH.
I THOUGHT YOU SAID THERE WOULDN'T BE ANY ROBIN COSTUMES!
RELAX, BOY WONDER...
...STEPHANIE'S GOT HER OWN BATGIRL COSTUME!
BATGIRL?
BUT I THOUGHT...
TOSS!
HUH?

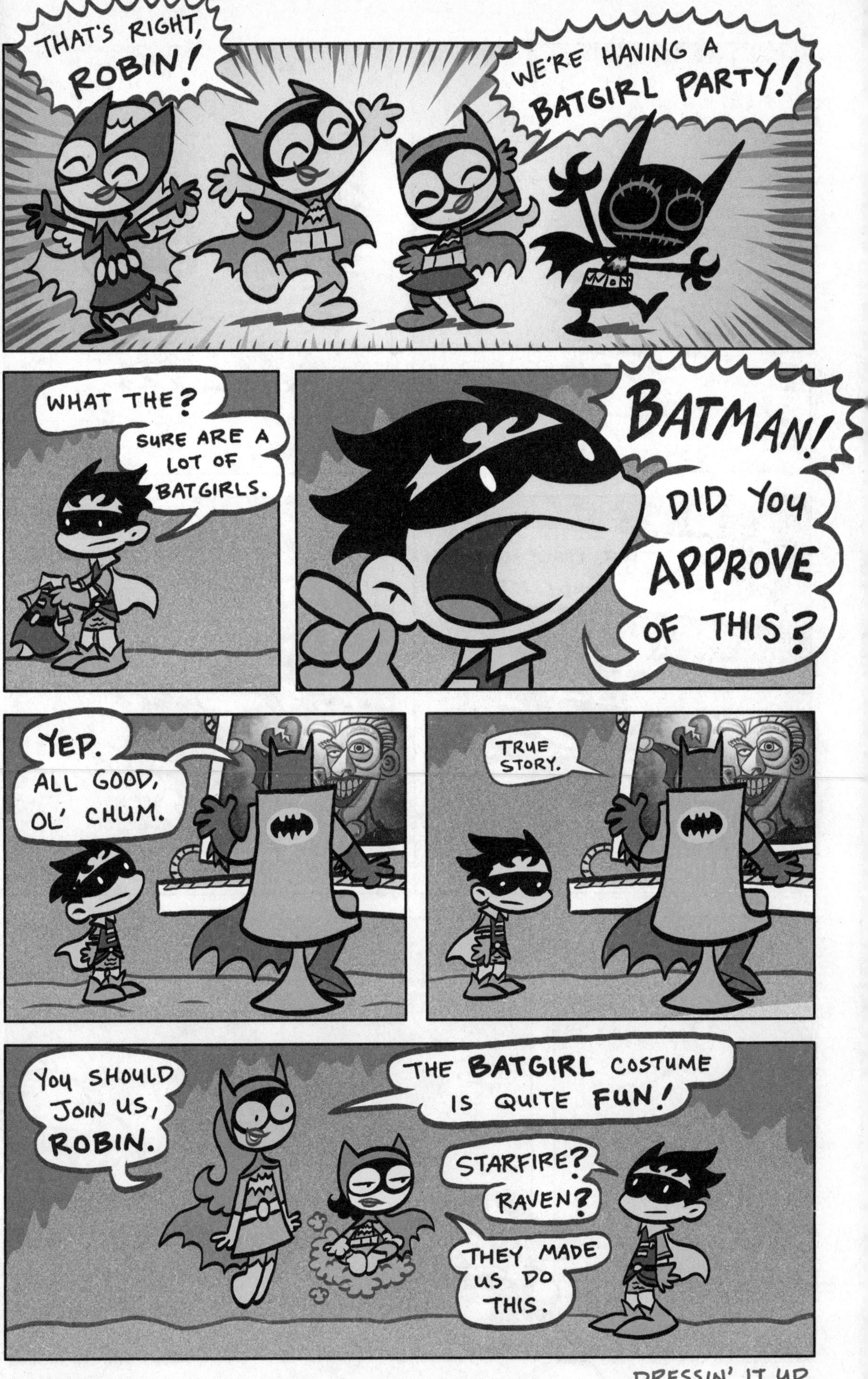
THAT'S RIGHT, ROBIN!
WE'RE HAVING A BATGIRL PARTY!
WHAT THE?
SURE ARE A LOT OF BATGIRLS.
BATMAN!
DID YOU APPROVE OF THIS?
YEP. ALL GOOD, OL' CHUM.
TRUE STORY.
YOU SHOULD JOIN US, ROBIN.
THE BATGIRL COSTUME IS QUITE FUN!
STARFIRE? RAVEN?
THEY MADE US DO THIS.

-DRESSIN' IT UP.

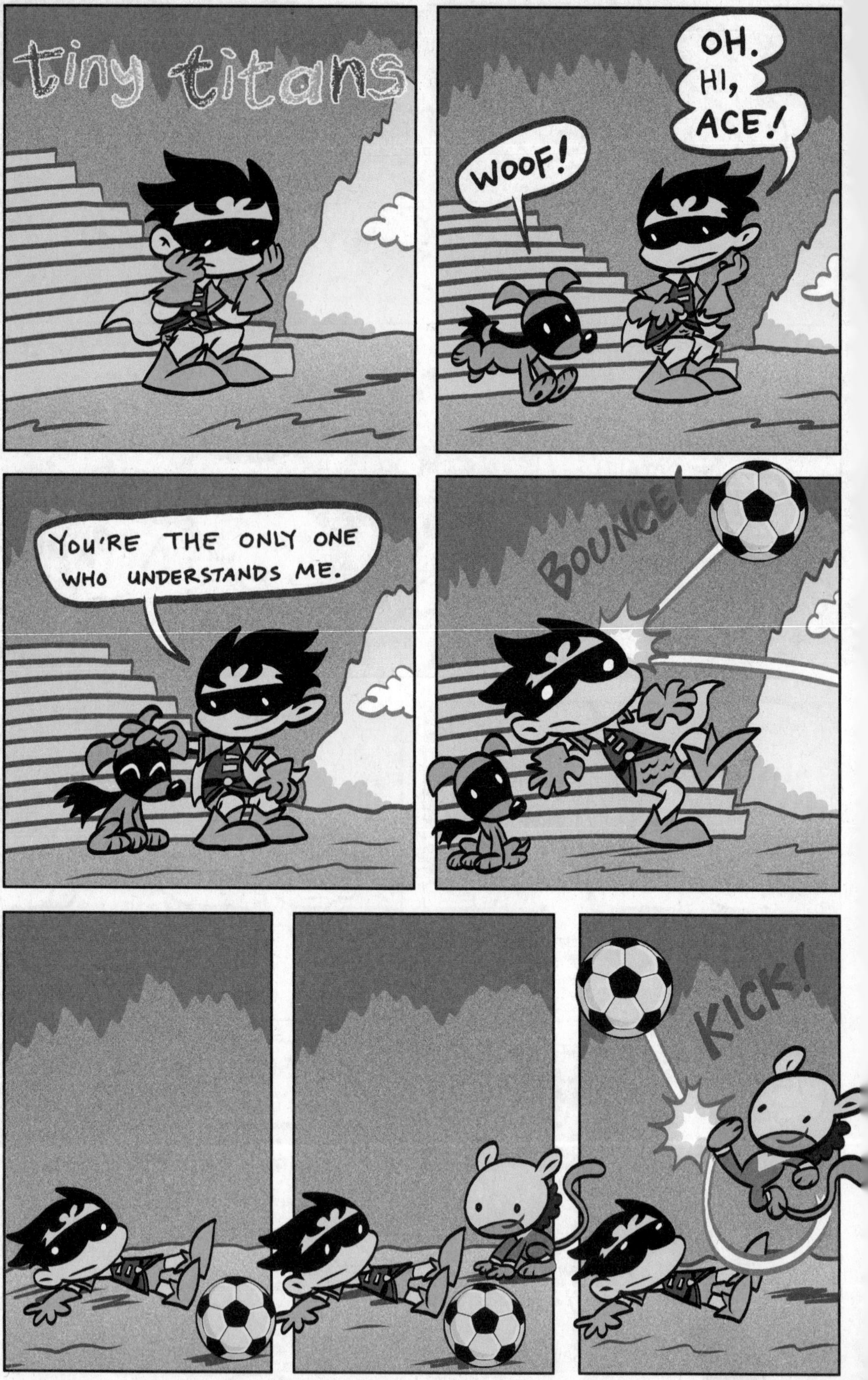
tiny titans
OH. HI, ACE!
WOOF!
YOU'RE THE ONLY ONE WHO UNDERSTANDS ME.
BOUNCE!
KICK!

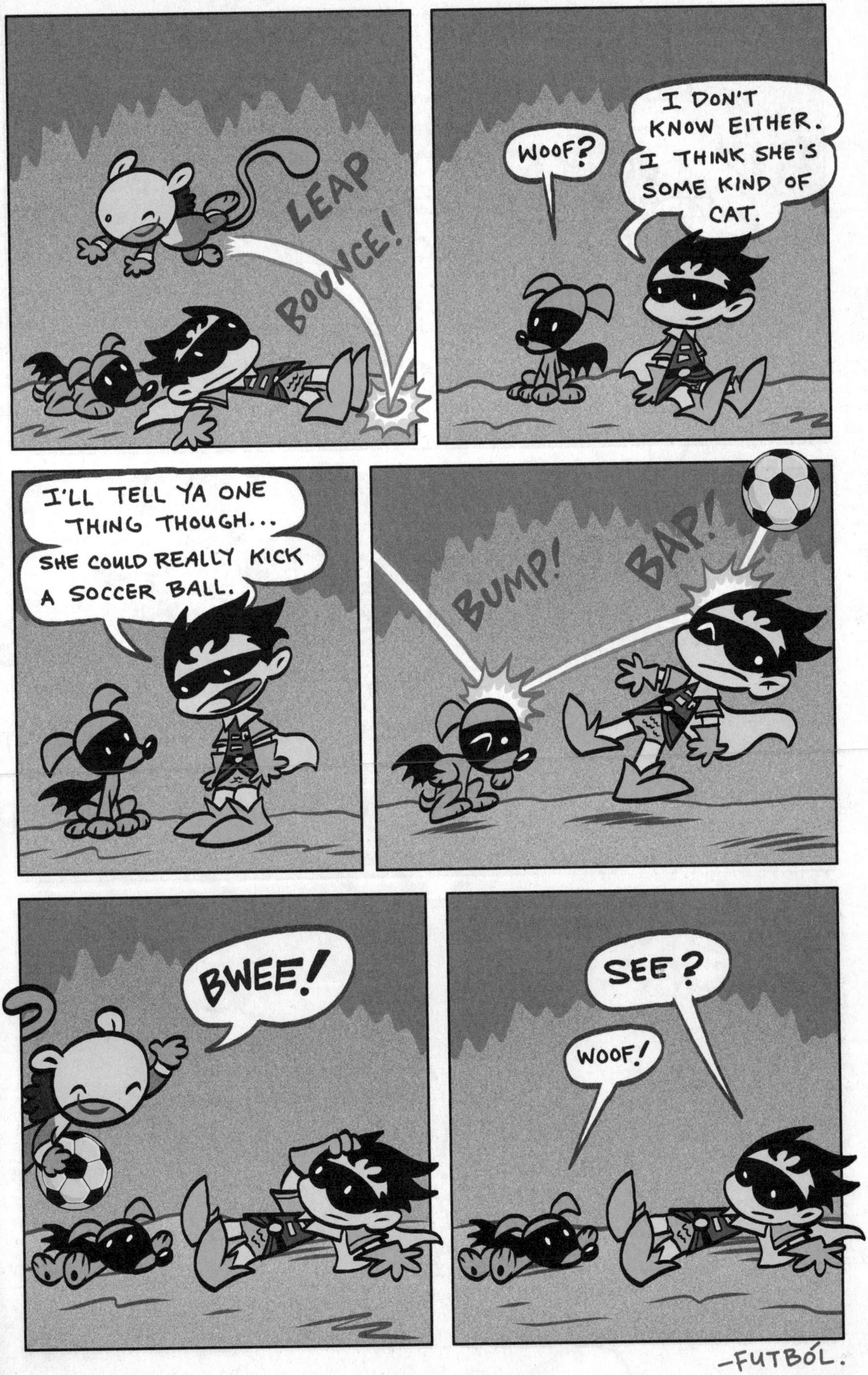
LEAP
BOUNCE!
WOOF?
I DON'T KNOW EITHER. I THINK SHE'S SOME KIND OF CAT.
I'LL TELL YA ONE THING THOUGH... SHE COULD REALLY KICK A SOCCER BALL.
BUMP!
BAP!
BWEE!
SEE?
WOOF!

-FUTBÓL.

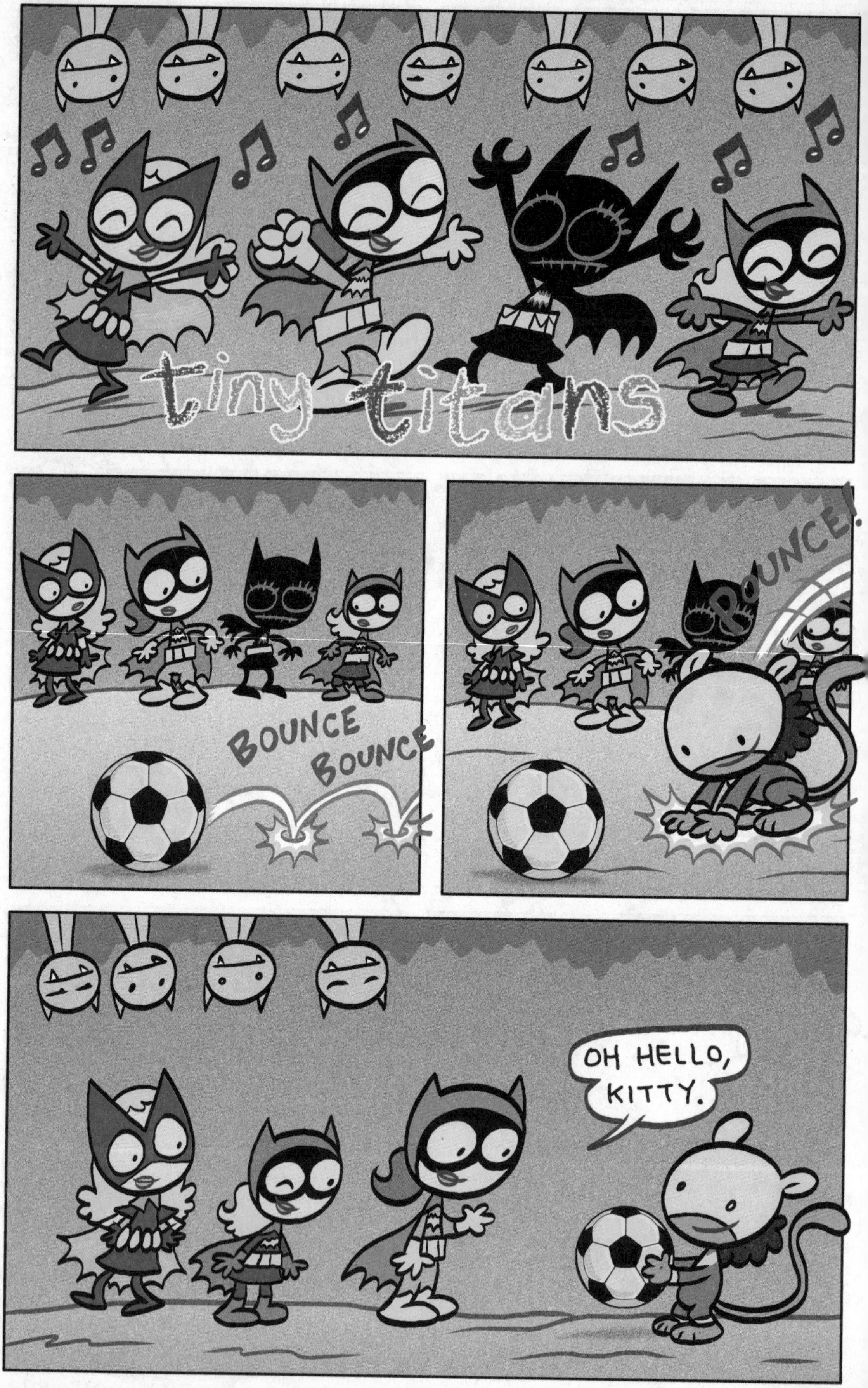
tiny titans
BOUNCE
BOUNCE
POUNCE!
OH HELLO, KITTY.

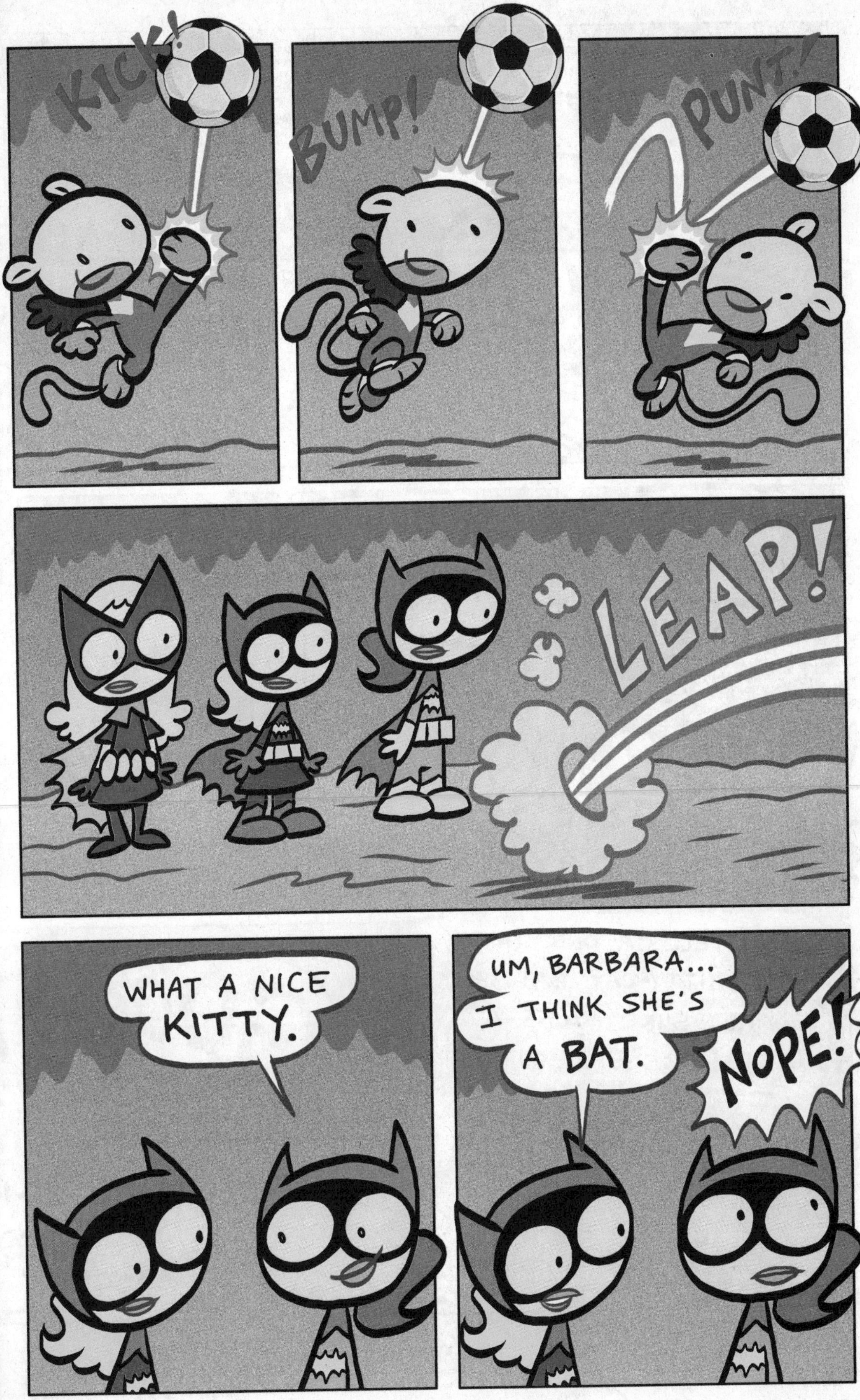
KICK!
BUMP!
PUNT!
LEAP!
WHAT A NICE KITTY.
UM, BARBARA... I THINK SHE'S A BAT.
NOPE!

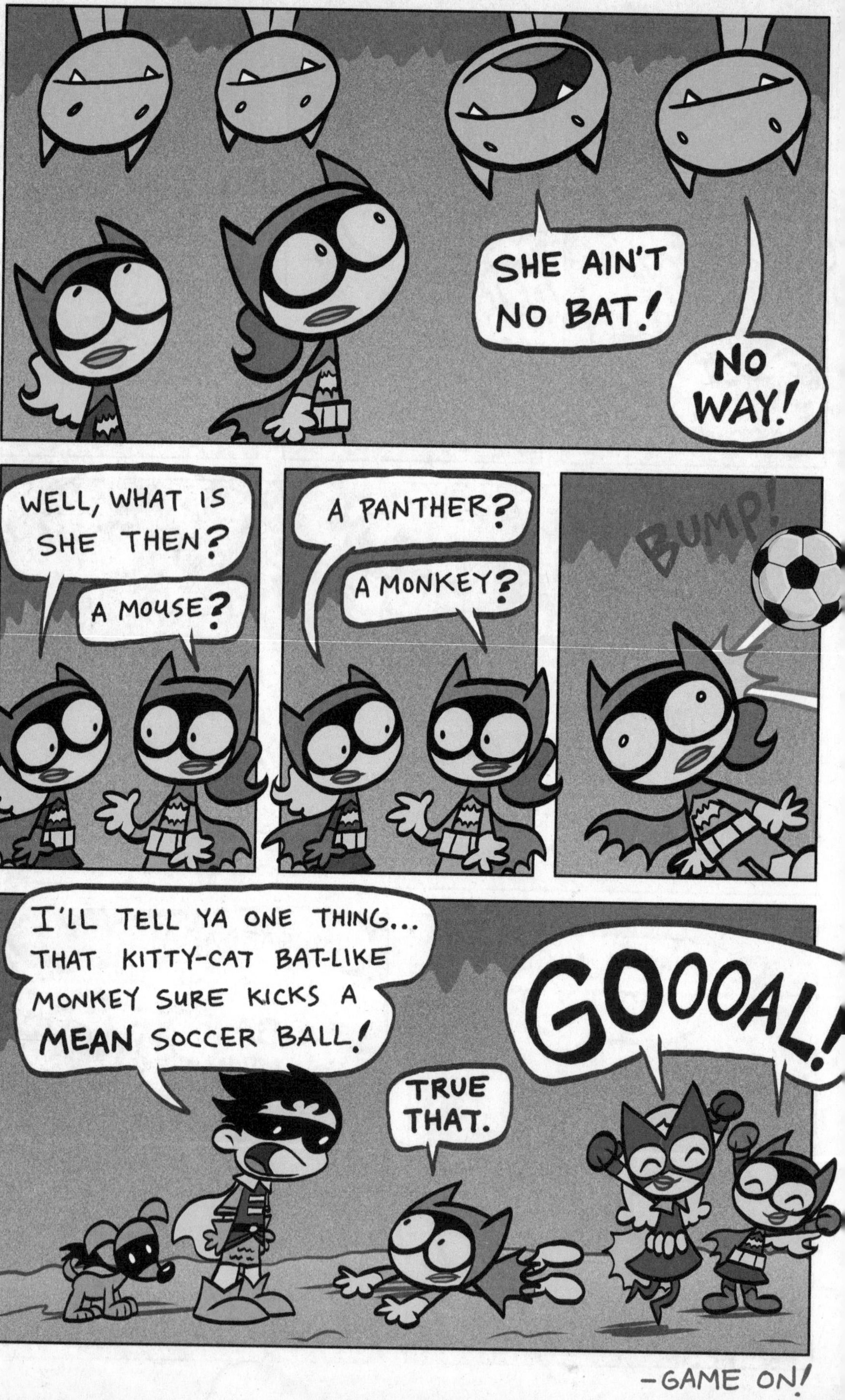
SHE AIN'T NO BAT!
NO WAY!
WELL, WHAT IS SHE THEN?
A MOUSE?
A PANTHER?
A MONKEY?
BUMP!
I'LL TELL YA ONE THING... THAT KITTY-CAT BAT-LIKE MONKEY SURE KICKS A MEAN SOCCER BALL!
TRUE THAT.
GOOOAL!

–GAME ON!

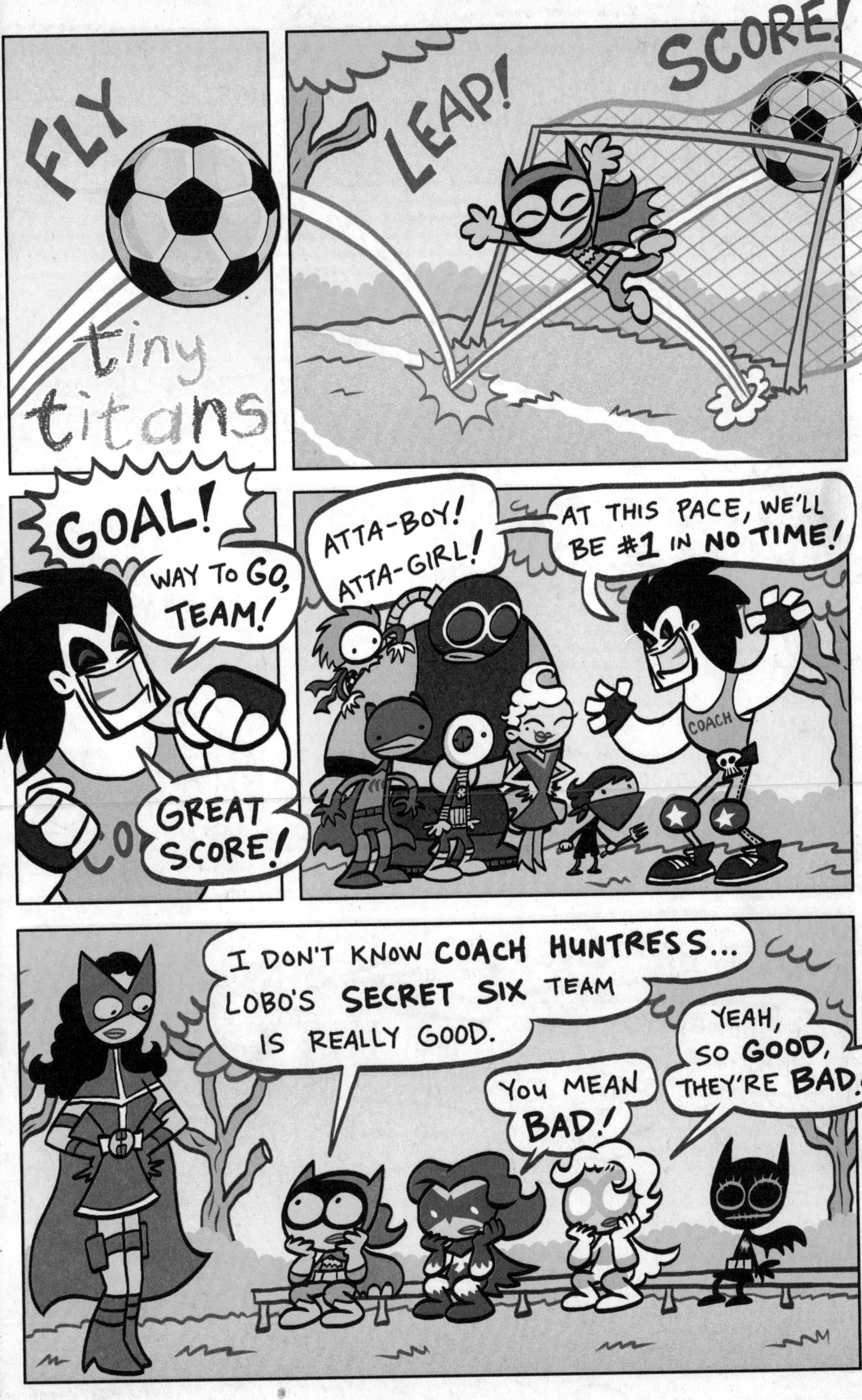
FLY
tiny titans
LEAP!
SCORE!
GOAL!
WAY TO GO, TEAM!
GREAT SCORE!
ATTA-BOY! ATTA-GIRL!
AT THIS PACE, WE'LL BE #1 IN NO TIME!
COACH
I DON'T KNOW COACH HUNTRESS... LOBO'S SECRET SIX TEAM IS REALLY GOOD.
YOU MEAN BAD!
YEAH, SO GOOD, THEY'RE BAD!

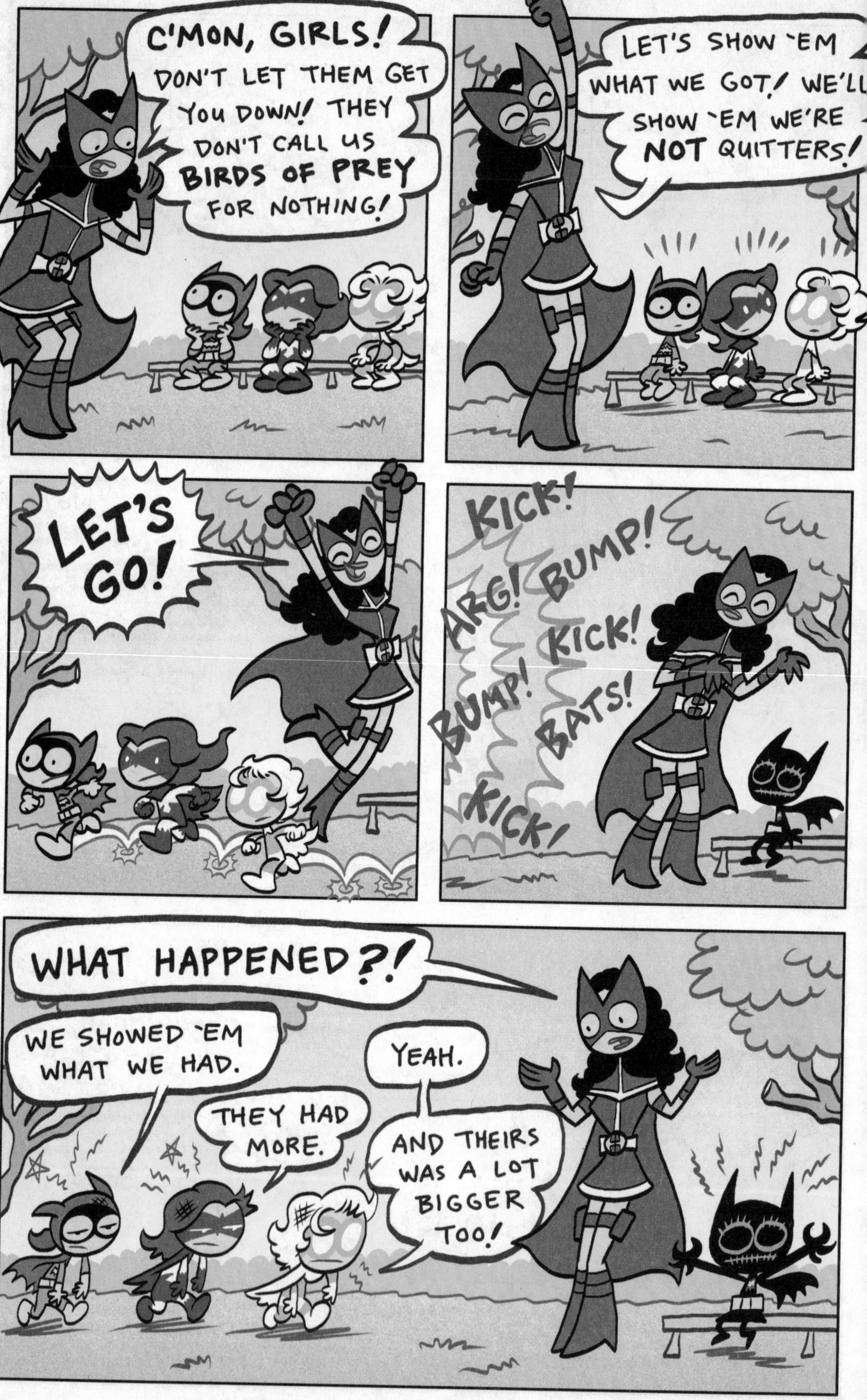
C'MON, GIRLS! DON'T LET THEM GET YOU DOWN! THEY DON'T CALL US BIRDS OF PREY FOR NOTHING!
LET'S SHOW 'EM WHAT WE GOT! WE'LL SHOW 'EM WE'RE NOT QUITTERS!
LET'S GO!
KICK!
BUMP!
ARG!
KICK!
BUMP!
BATS!
KICK!
WHAT HAPPENED?!
WE SHOWED 'EM WHAT WE HAD.
THEY HAD MORE.
YEAH.
AND THEIRS WAS A LOT BIGGER TOO!

—SIXTH SENSE.

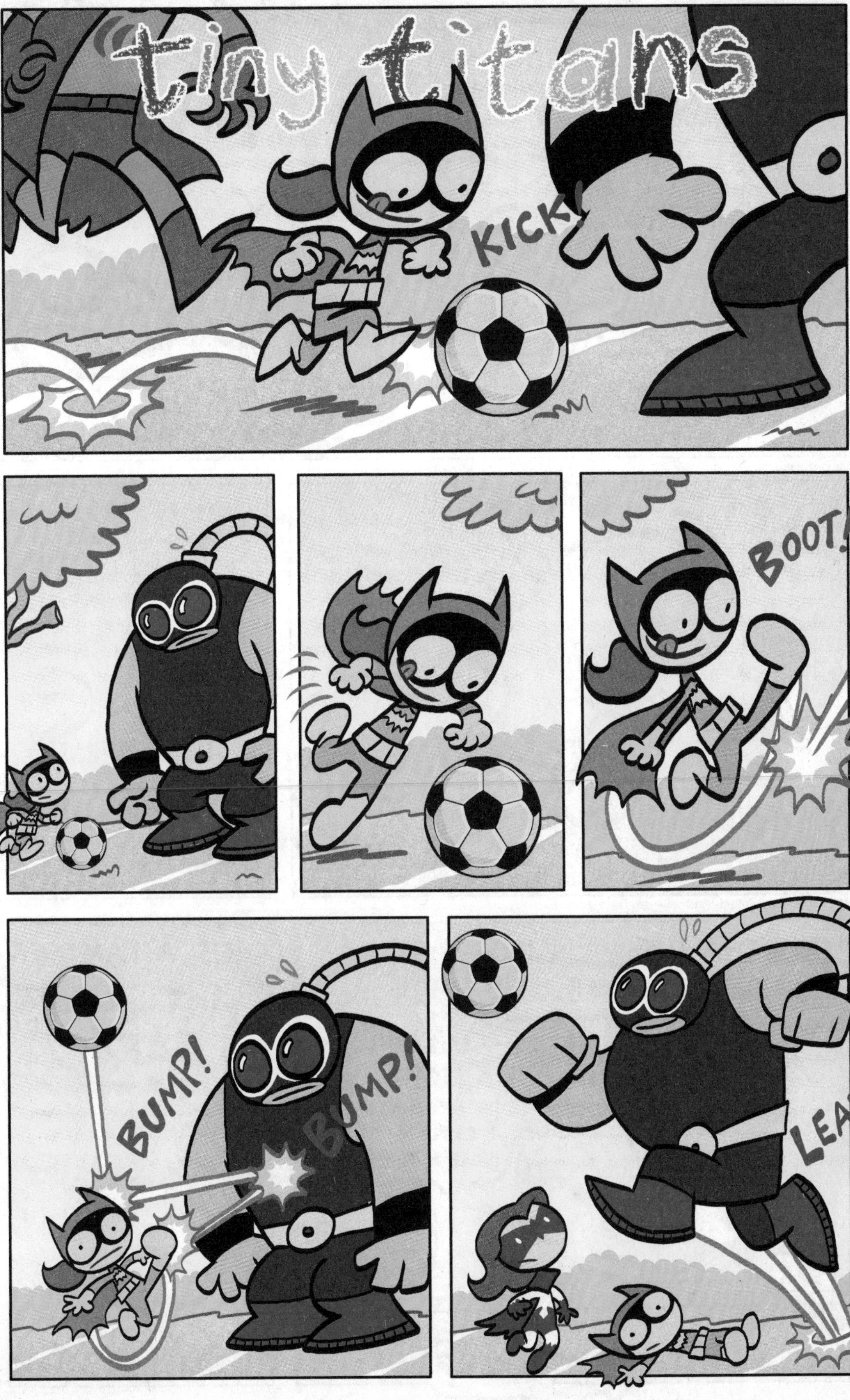
tiny titans
KICK!
BOOT!
BUMP!
BUMP!
LEAP!

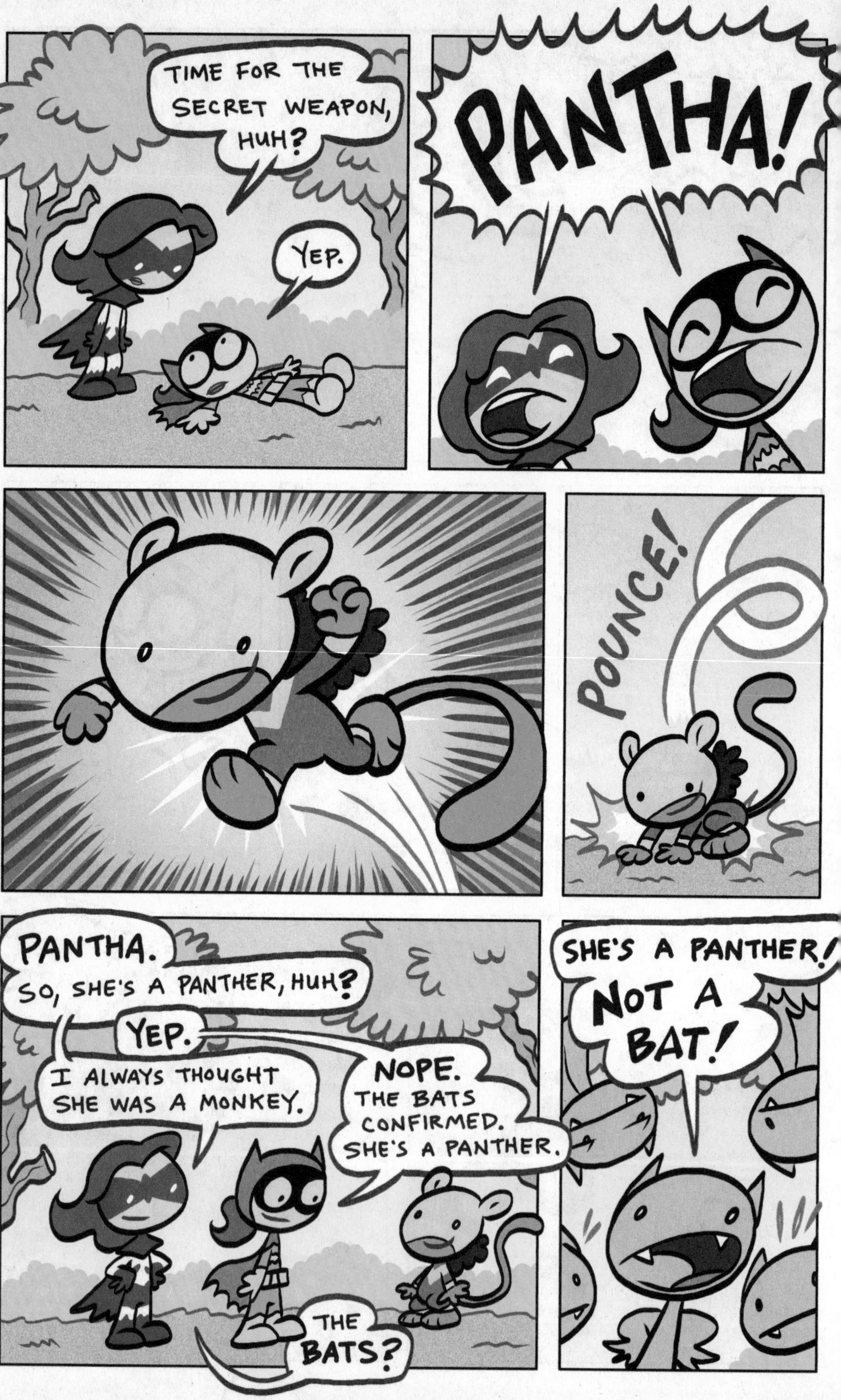
TIME FOR THE SECRET WEAPON, HUH?
YEP.
PANTHA!
POUNCE!
PANTHA.
SO, SHE'S A PANTHER, HUH?
YEP.
I ALWAYS THOUGHT SHE WAS A MONKEY.
NOPE. THE BATS CONFIRMED. SHE'S A PANTHER.
THE BATS?
SHE'S A PANTHER!
NOT A BAT!

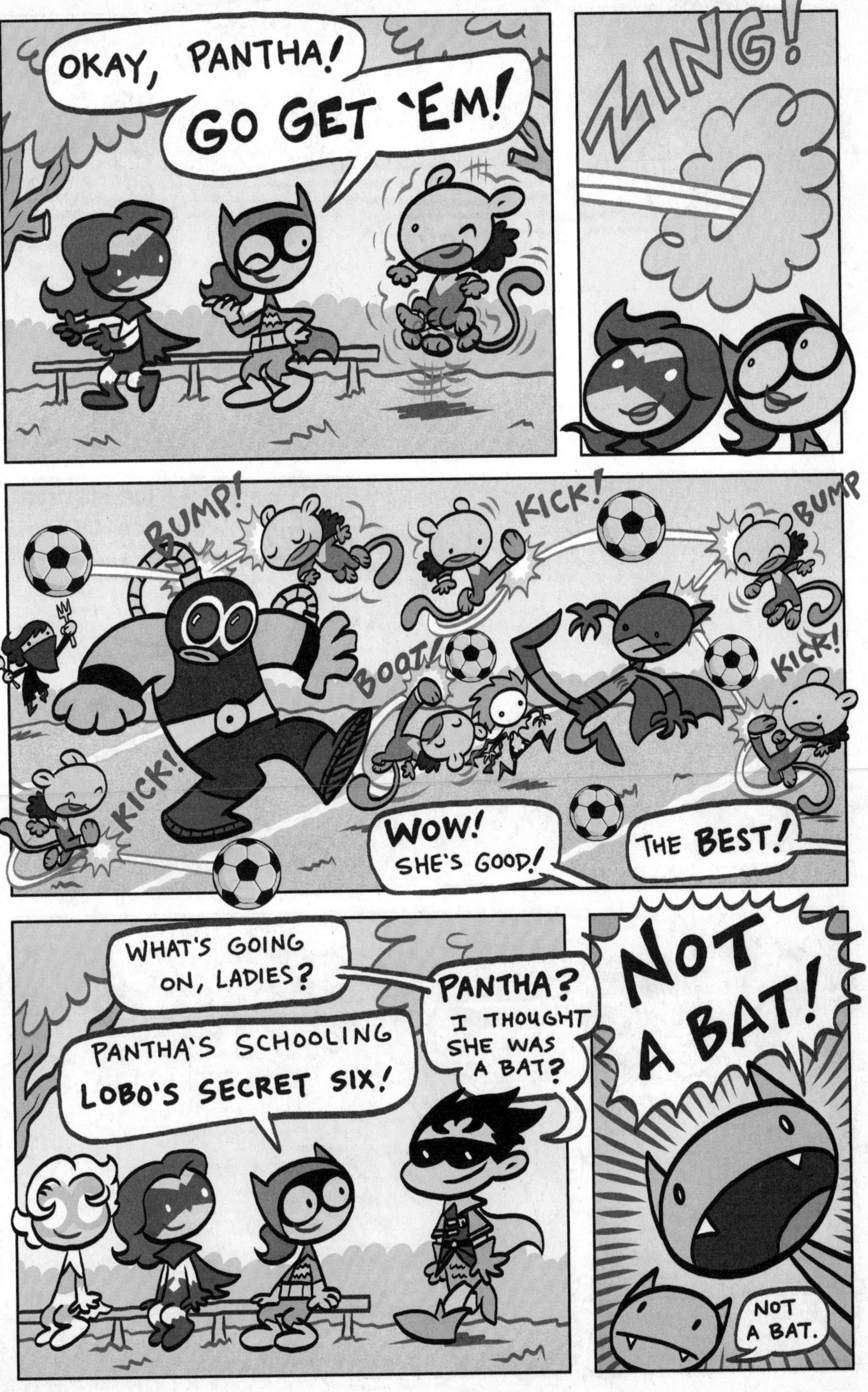
OKAY, PANTHA! GO GET 'EM!
ZING!
BUMP!
KICK!
BUMP
BOOT!
KICK!
KICK!
WOW! SHE'S GOOD!
THE BEST!
WHAT'S GOING ON, LADIES?
PANTHA'S SCHOOLING LOBO'S SECRET SIX!
PANTHA? I THOUGHT SHE WAS A BAT?
NOT A BAT!
NOT A BAT.

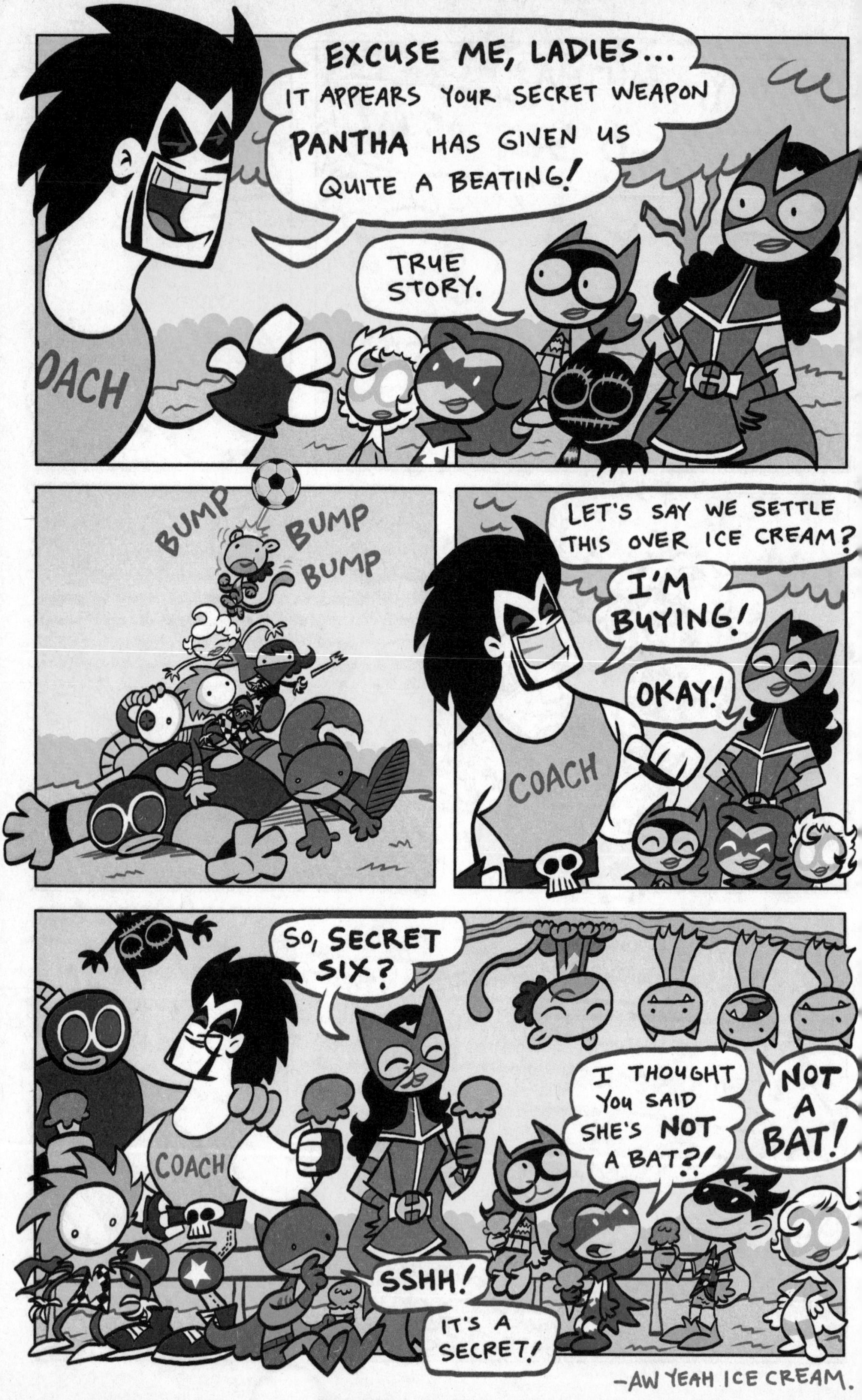
EXCUSE ME, LADIES... IT APPEARS YOUR SECRET WEAPON PANTHA HAS GIVEN US QUITE A BEATING!
TRUE STORY.
COACH
BUMP
BUMP
BUMP
LET'S SAY WE SETTLE THIS OVER ICE CREAM?
I'M BUYING!
OKAY!
COACH
SO, SECRET SIX?
COACH
I THOUGHT YOU SAID SHE'S NOT A BAT?!
NOT A BAT!
SSHH!
IT'S A SECRET!

—AW YEAH ICE CREAM.

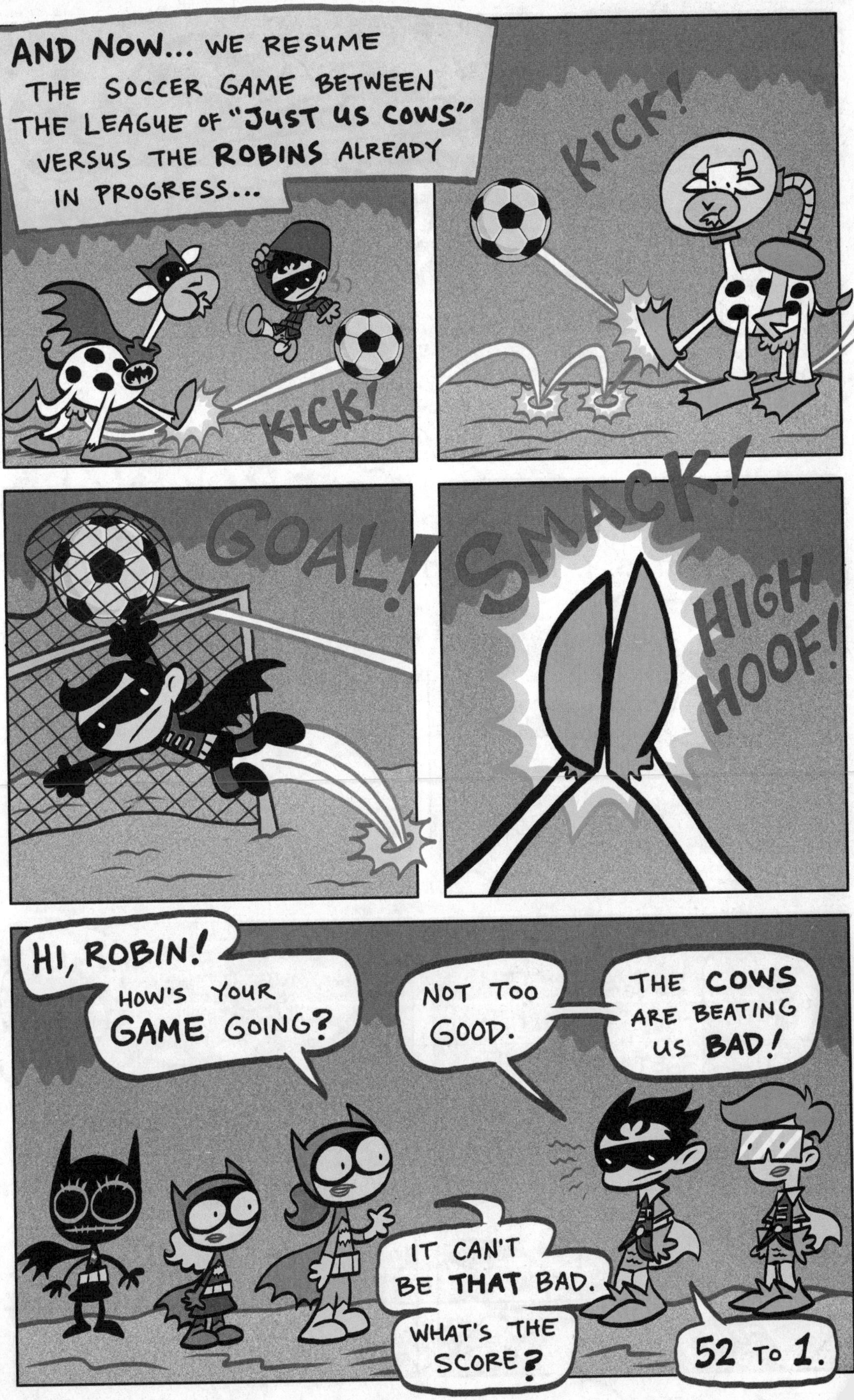

AND NOW... WE RESUME THE SOCCER GAME BETWEEN THE LEAGUE OF "JUST US COWS" VERSUS THE ROBINS ALREADY IN PROGRESS...
KICK!
KICK!
GOAL!
SMACK!
HIGH HOOF!
HI, ROBIN! HOW'S YOUR GAME GOING?
NOT TOO GOOD.
THE COWS ARE BEATING US BAD!
IT CAN'T BE THAT BAD.
WHAT'S THE SCORE?
52 TO 1.

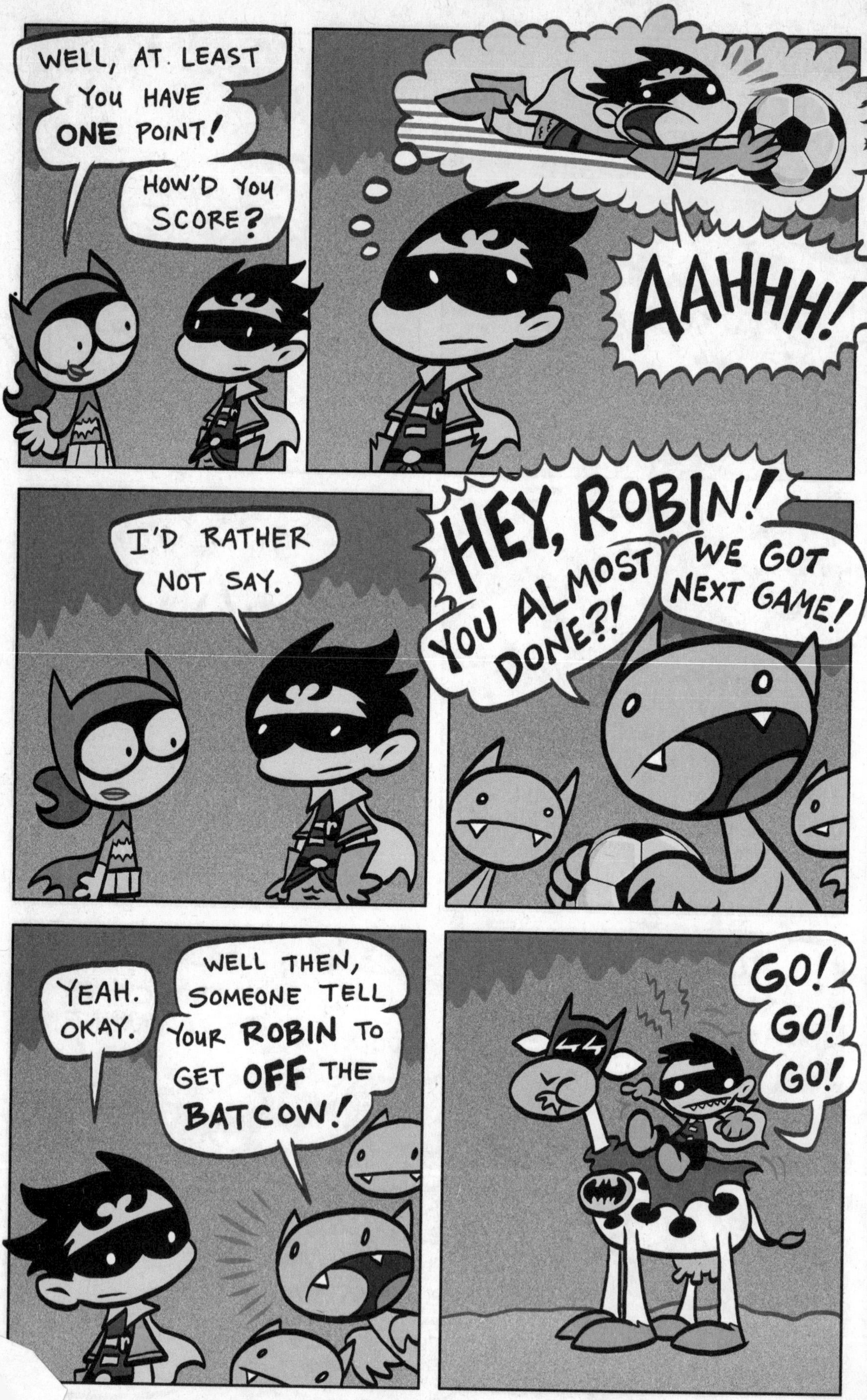

WELL, AT LEAST YOU HAVE ONE POINT!
HOW'D YOU SCORE?
AAHHH!
I'D RATHER NOT SAY.
HEY, ROBIN!
YOU ALMOST DONE?!
WE GOT NEXT GAME!
YEAH. OKAY.
WELL THEN, SOMEONE TELL YOUR ROBIN TO GET OFF THE BATCOW!
GO! GO! GO!

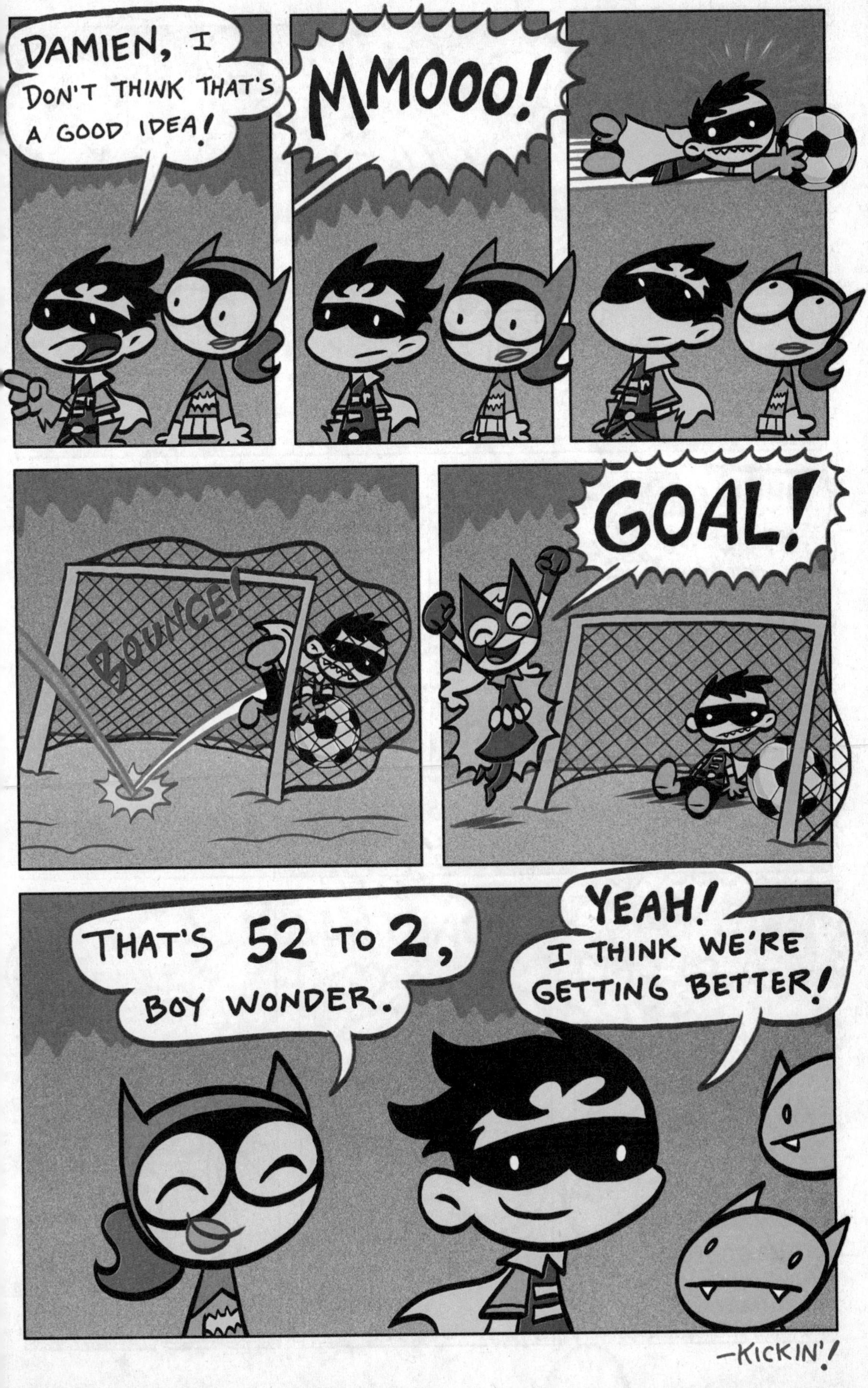
DAMIEN, I DON'T THINK THAT'S A GOOD IDEA!
MMOOO!
BOUNCE!
GOAL!
THAT'S 52 TO 2, BOY WONDER.
YEAH! I THINK WE'RE GETTING BETTER!
—KICKIN'!

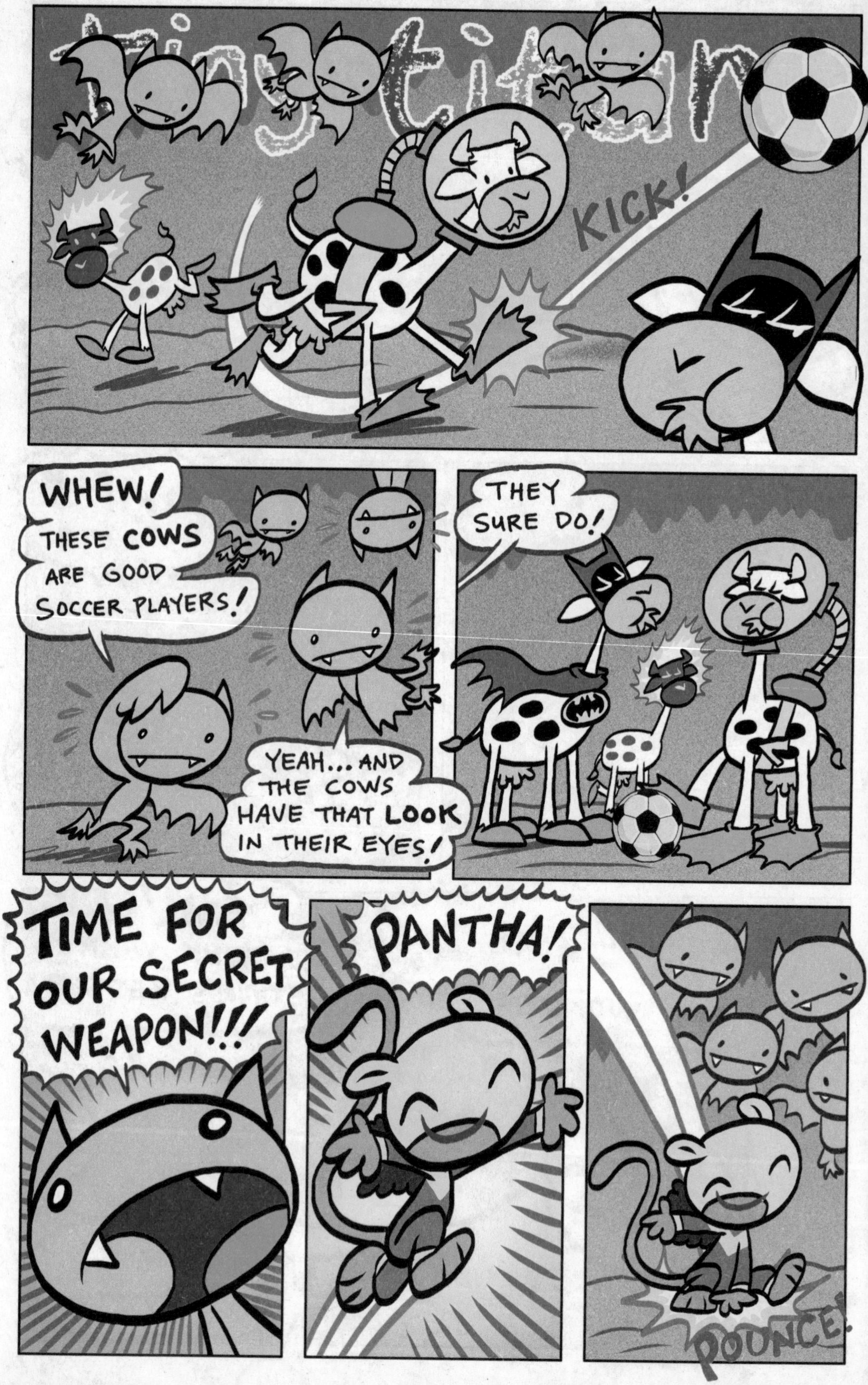
tiny titan
KICK!
WHEW! THESE COWS ARE GOOD SOCCER PLAYERS!
YEAH... AND THE COWS HAVE THAT LOOK IN THEIR EYES!
THEY SURE DO!
TIME FOR OUR SECRET WEAPON!!!
PANTHA!
POUNCE!

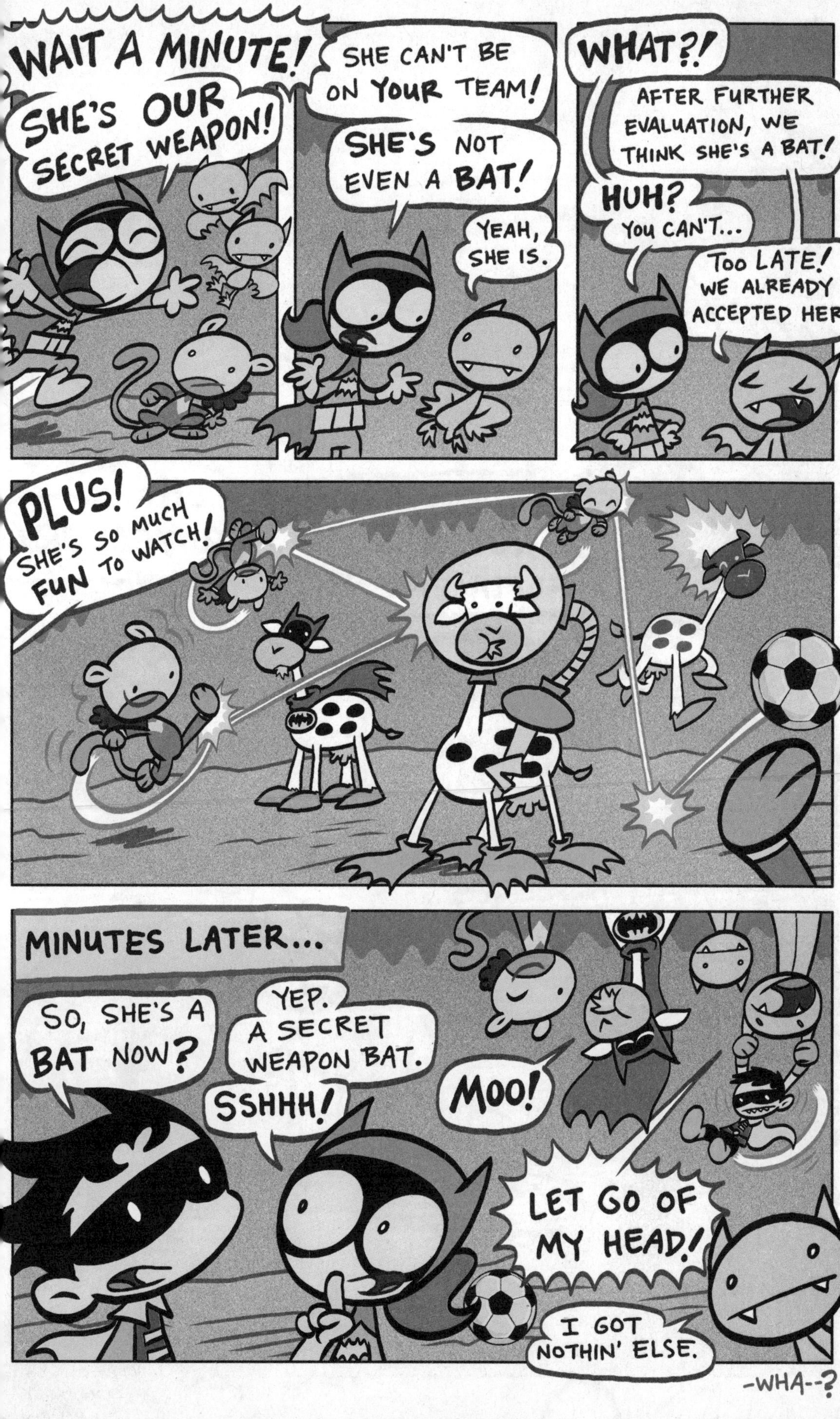
WAIT A MINUTE!
SHE'S OUR SECRET WEAPON!
SHE CAN'T BE ON YOUR TEAM!
SHE'S NOT EVEN A BAT!
YEAH, SHE IS.
WHAT?!
AFTER FURTHER EVALUATION, WE THINK SHE'S A BAT!
HUH? YOU CAN'T...
TOO LATE! WE ALREADY ACCEPTED HER!
PLUS! SHE'S SO MUCH FUN TO WATCH!
MINUTES LATER...
SO, SHE'S A BAT NOW?
YEP. A SECRET WEAPON BAT.
SSHHH!
MOO!
LET GO OF MY HEAD!
I GOT NOTHIN' ELSE.
-WHA--?

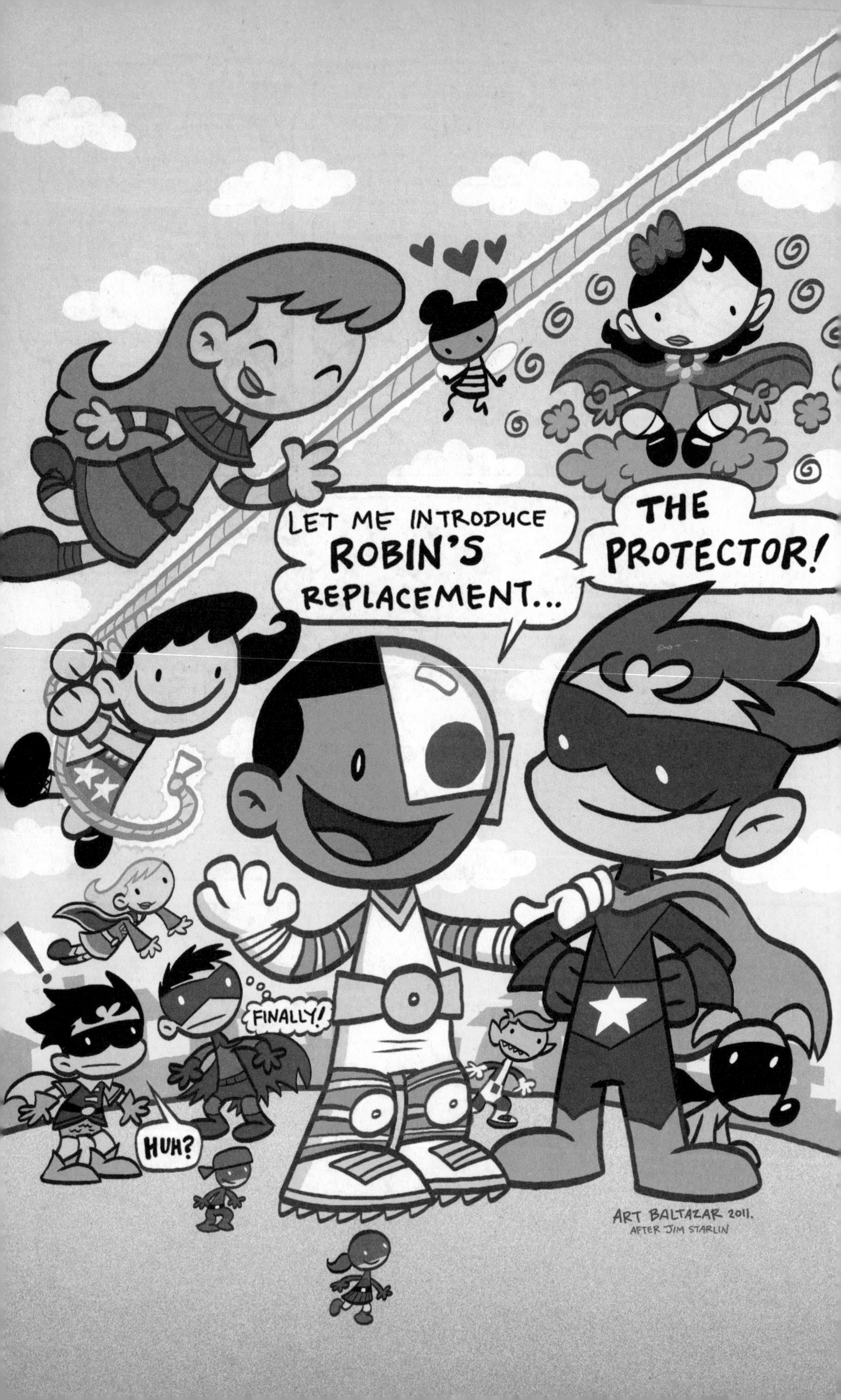
LET ME INTRODUCE ROBIN'S REPLACEMENT...
THE PROTECTOR!
!
FINALLY!
HUH?
ART BALTAZAR 2011.
AFTER JIM STARLIN

tiny titans

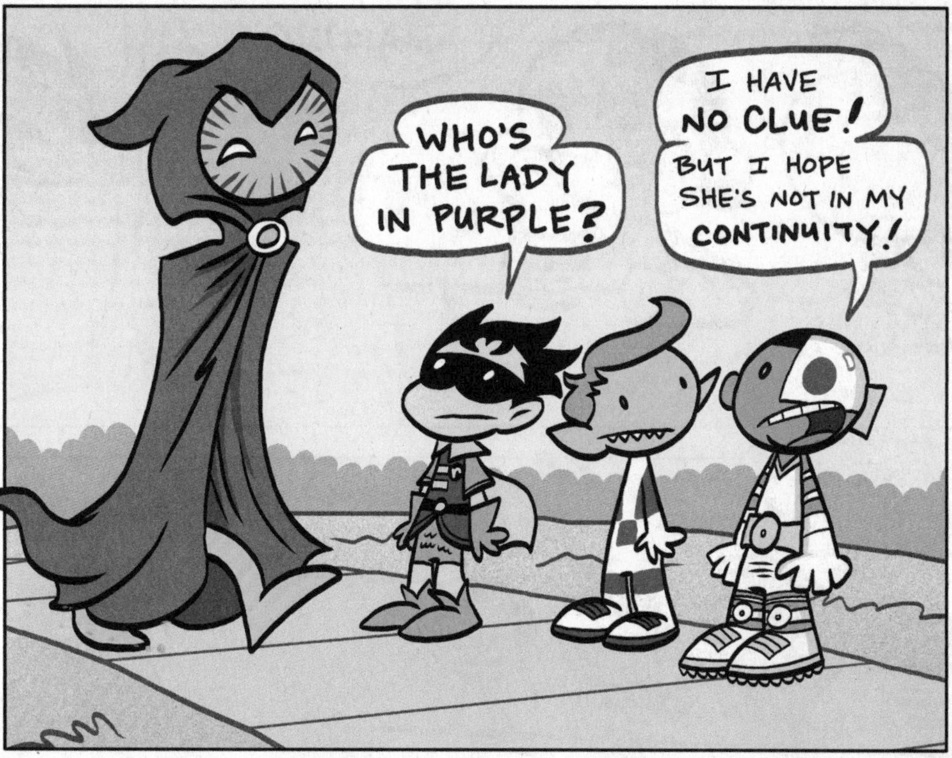
WHO'S THE LADY IN PURPLE?
I HAVE NO CLUE! BUT I HOPE SHE'S NOT IN MY CONTINUITY!

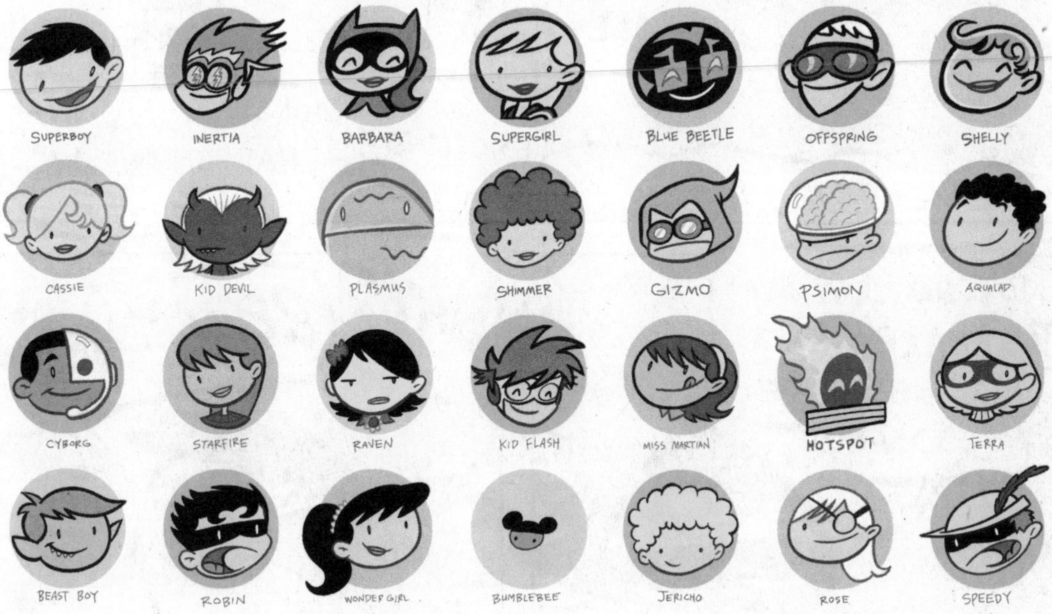
SUPERBOY
INERTIA
BARBARA
SUPERGIRL
BLUE BEETLE
OFFSPRING
SHELLY
CASSIE
KID DEVIL
PLASMUS
SHIMMER
GIZMO
PSIMON
AQUALAD
CYBORG
STARFIRE
RAVEN
KID FLASH
MISS MARTIAN
HOTSPOT
TERRA
BEAST BOY
ROBIN
WONDER GIRL
BUMBLEBEE
JERICHO
ROSE
SPEEDY

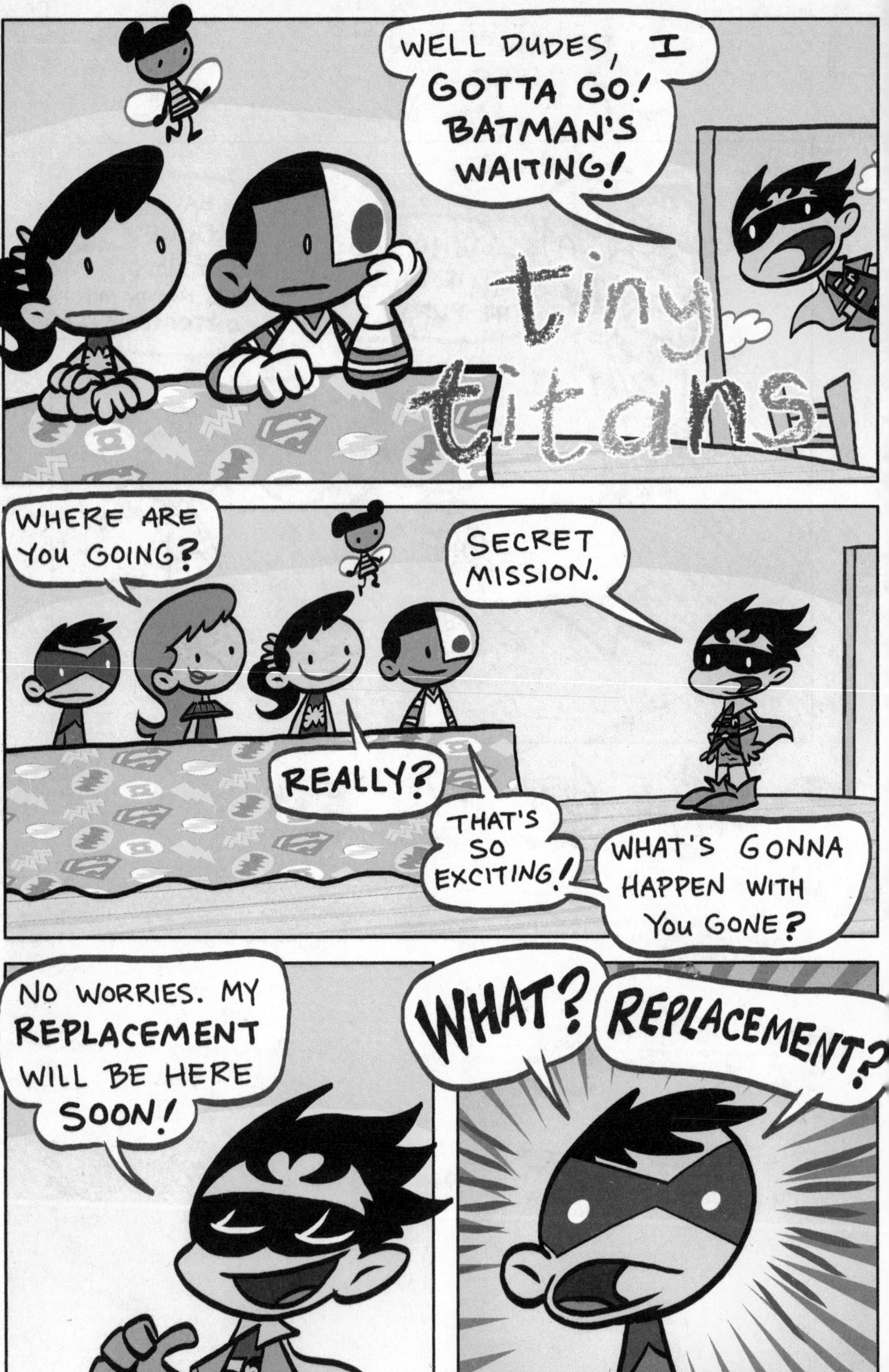
WELL DUDES, I GOTTA GO! BATMAN'S WAITING!
tiny titans
WHERE ARE YOU GOING?
SECRET MISSION.
REALLY?
THAT'S SO EXCITING!
WHAT'S GONNA HAPPEN WITH YOU GONE?
NO WORRIES. MY REPLACEMENT WILL BE HERE SOON!
WHAT?
REPLACEMENT?

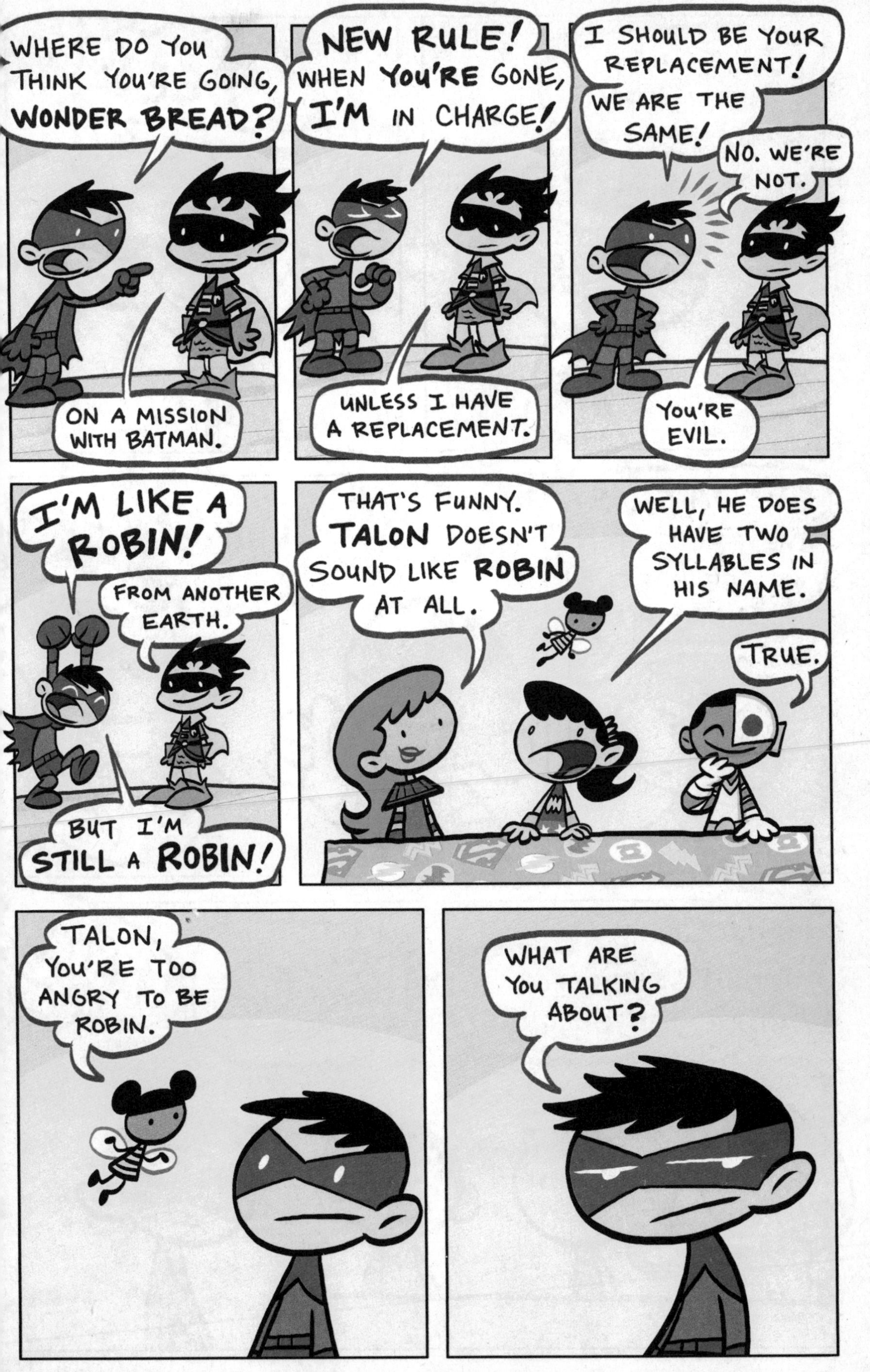
WHERE DO YOU THINK YOU'RE GOING, WONDER BREAD?
ON A MISSION WITH BATMAN.
NEW RULE! WHEN YOU'RE GONE, I'M IN CHARGE!
UNLESS I HAVE A REPLACEMENT.
I SHOULD BE YOUR REPLACEMENT!
WE ARE THE SAME!
NO. WE'RE NOT.
YOU'RE EVIL.
I'M LIKE A ROBIN!
FROM ANOTHER EARTH.
BUT I'M STILL A ROBIN!
THAT'S FUNNY. TALON DOESN'T SOUND LIKE ROBIN AT ALL.
WELL, HE DOES HAVE TWO SYLLABLES IN HIS NAME.
TRUE.
TALON, YOU'RE TOO ANGRY TO BE ROBIN.
WHAT ARE YOU TALKING ABOUT?

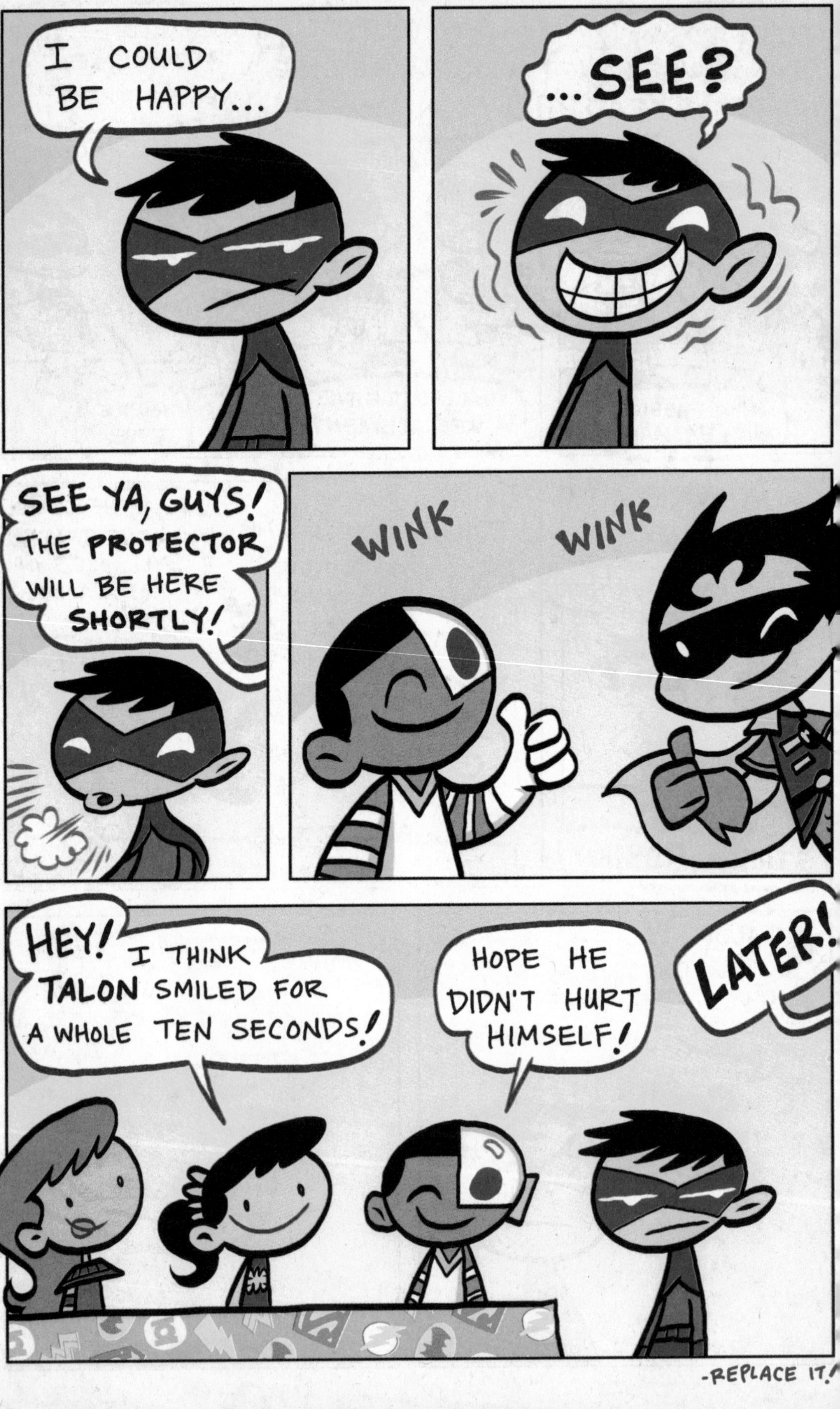
I COULD BE HAPPY...
...SEE?
SEE YA, GUYS! THE PROTECTOR WILL BE HERE SHORTLY!
WINK
WINK
HEY! I THINK TALON SMILED FOR A WHOLE TEN SECONDS!
HOPE HE DIDN'T HURT HIMSELF!
LATER!
-REPLACE IT!

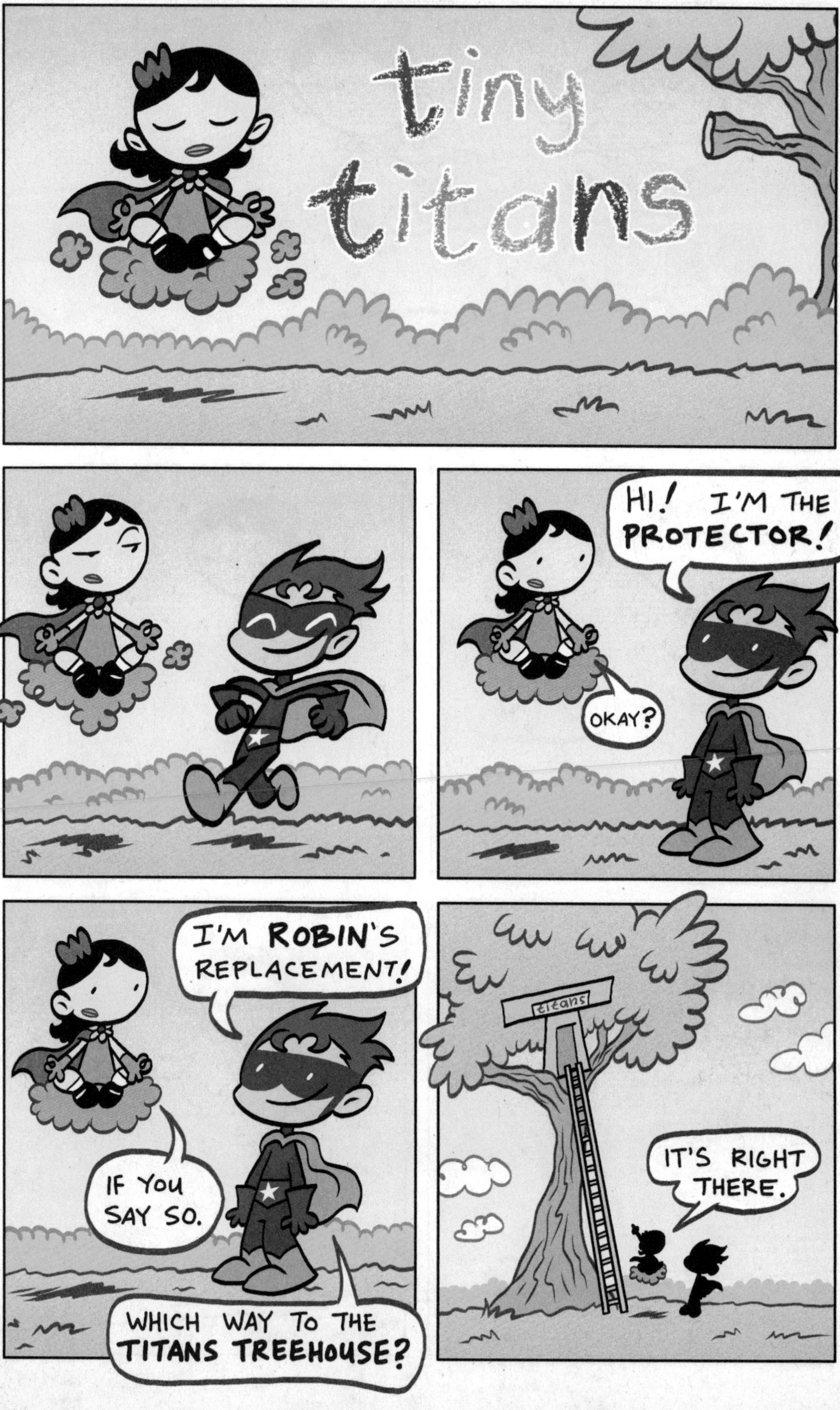
tiny titans
HI! I'M THE PROTECTOR!
OKAY?
I'M ROBIN'S REPLACEMENT!
IF YOU SAY SO.
WHICH WAY TO THE TITANS TREEHOUSE?
titans
IT'S RIGHT THERE.

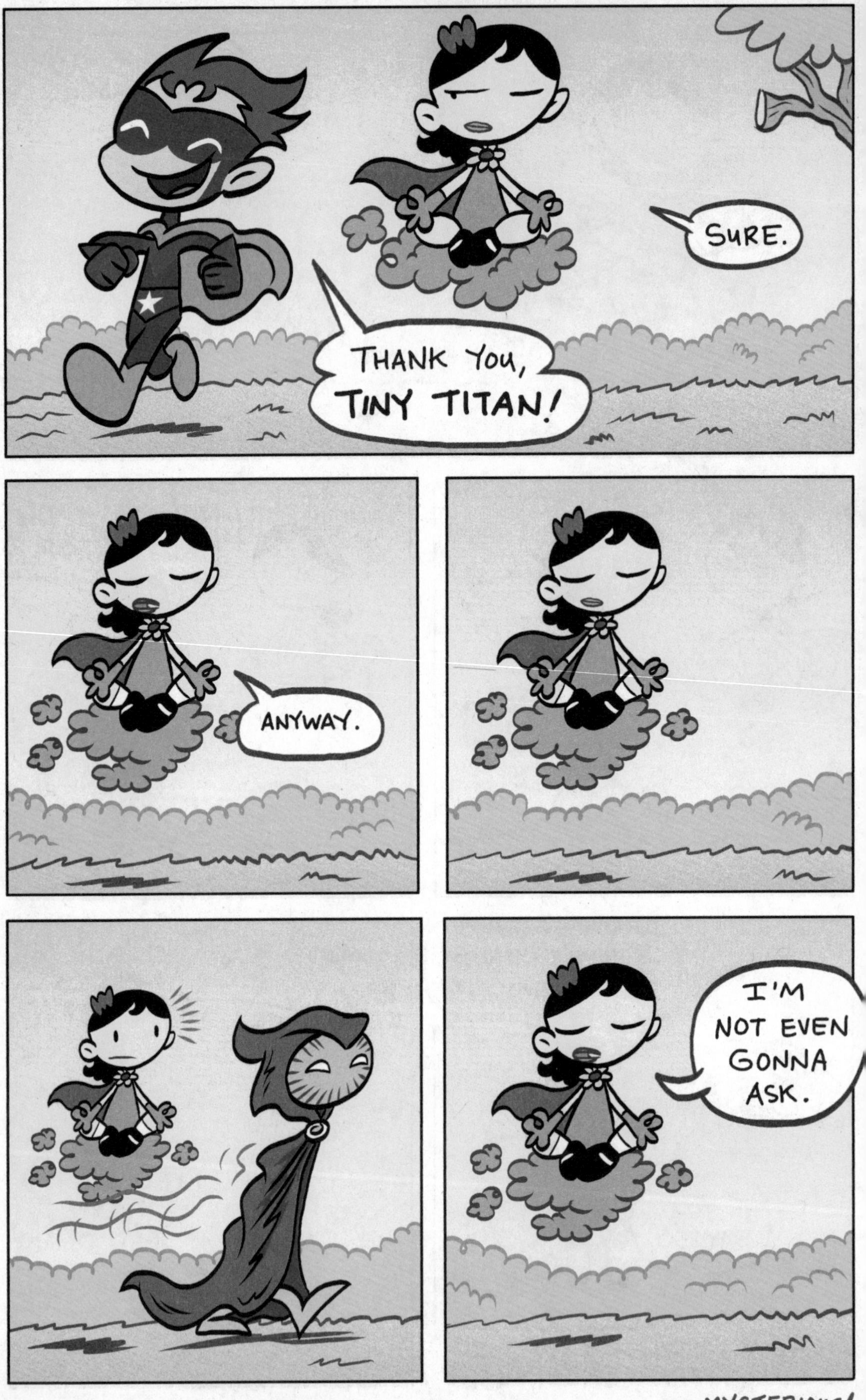
SURE.
THANK YOU, TINY TITAN!
ANYWAY.
I'M NOT EVEN GONNA ASK.

—MYSTERIOUS!

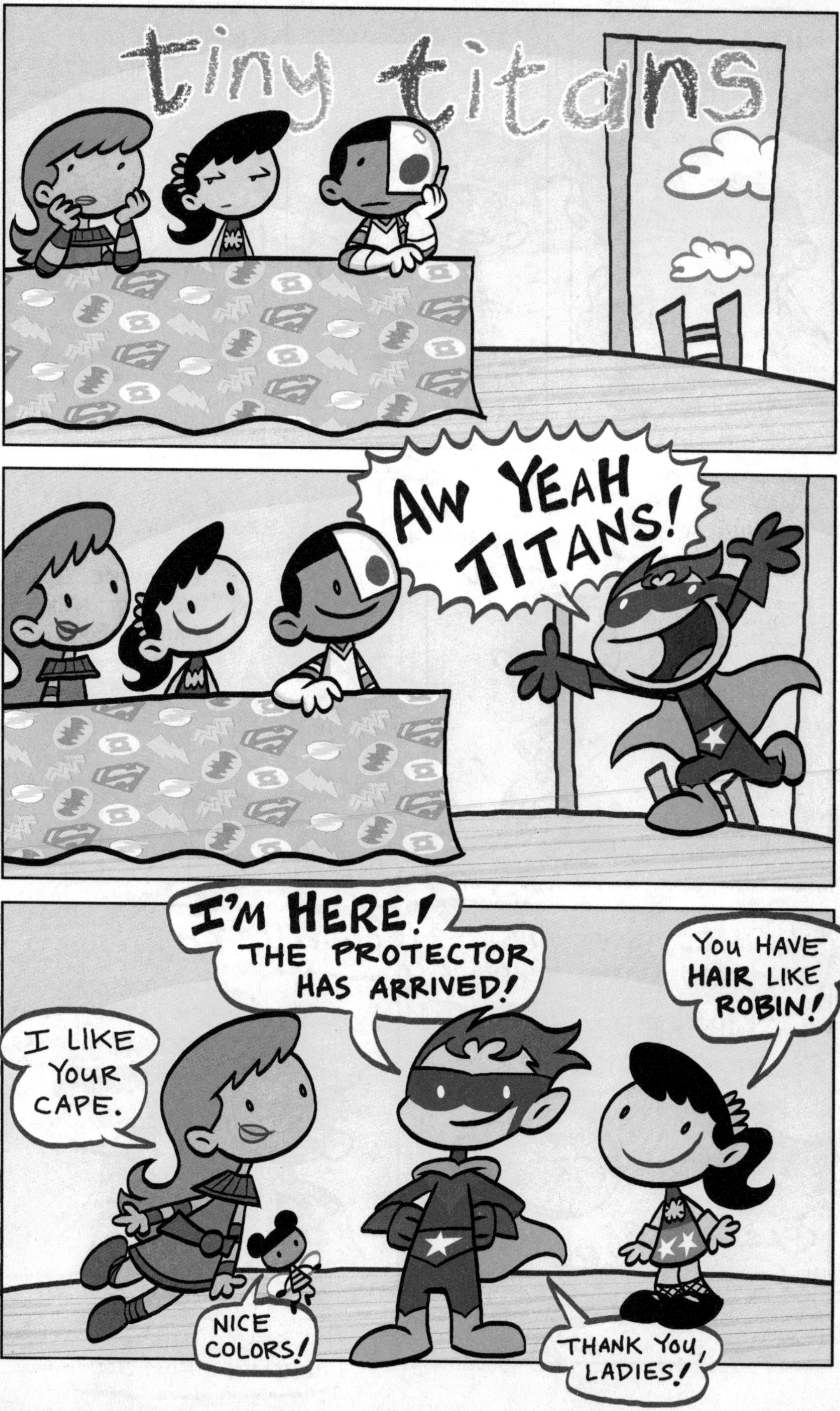
tiny titans
AW YEAH TITANS!
I'M HERE! THE PROTECTOR HAS ARRIVED!
I LIKE YOUR CAPE.
YOU HAVE HAIR LIKE ROBIN!
NICE COLORS!
THANK YOU, LADIES!

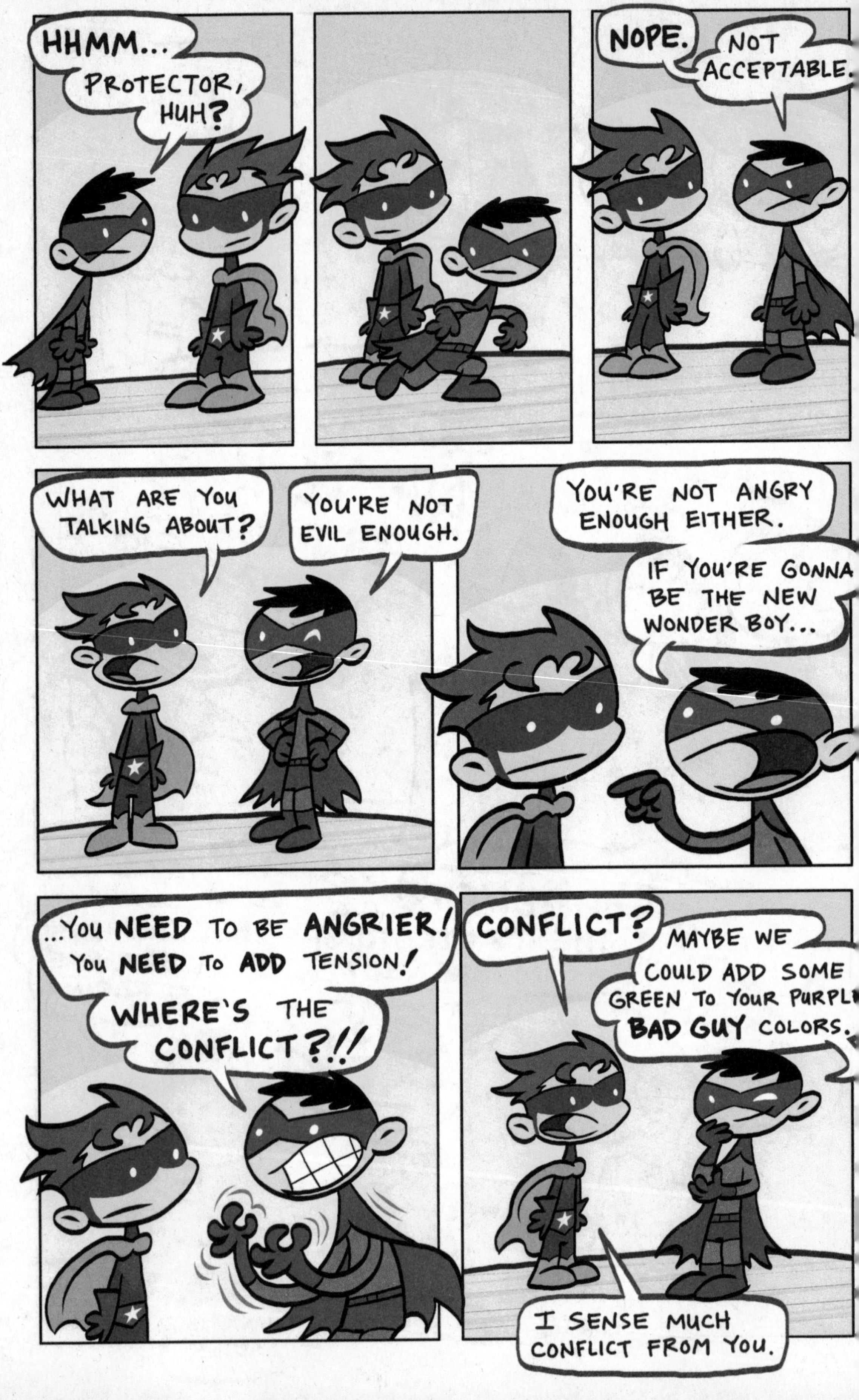
HHMM...
PROTECTOR, HUH?
NOPE.
NOT ACCEPTABLE.
WHAT ARE YOU TALKING ABOUT?
YOU'RE NOT EVIL ENOUGH.
YOU'RE NOT ANGRY ENOUGH EITHER.
IF YOU'RE GONNA BE THE NEW WONDER BOY...
...YOU NEED TO BE ANGRIER! YOU NEED TO ADD TENSION!
WHERE'S THE CONFLICT?!!
CONFLICT?
MAYBE WE COULD ADD SOME GREEN TO YOUR PURPL BAD GUY COLORS.
I SENSE MUCH CONFLICT FROM YOU.

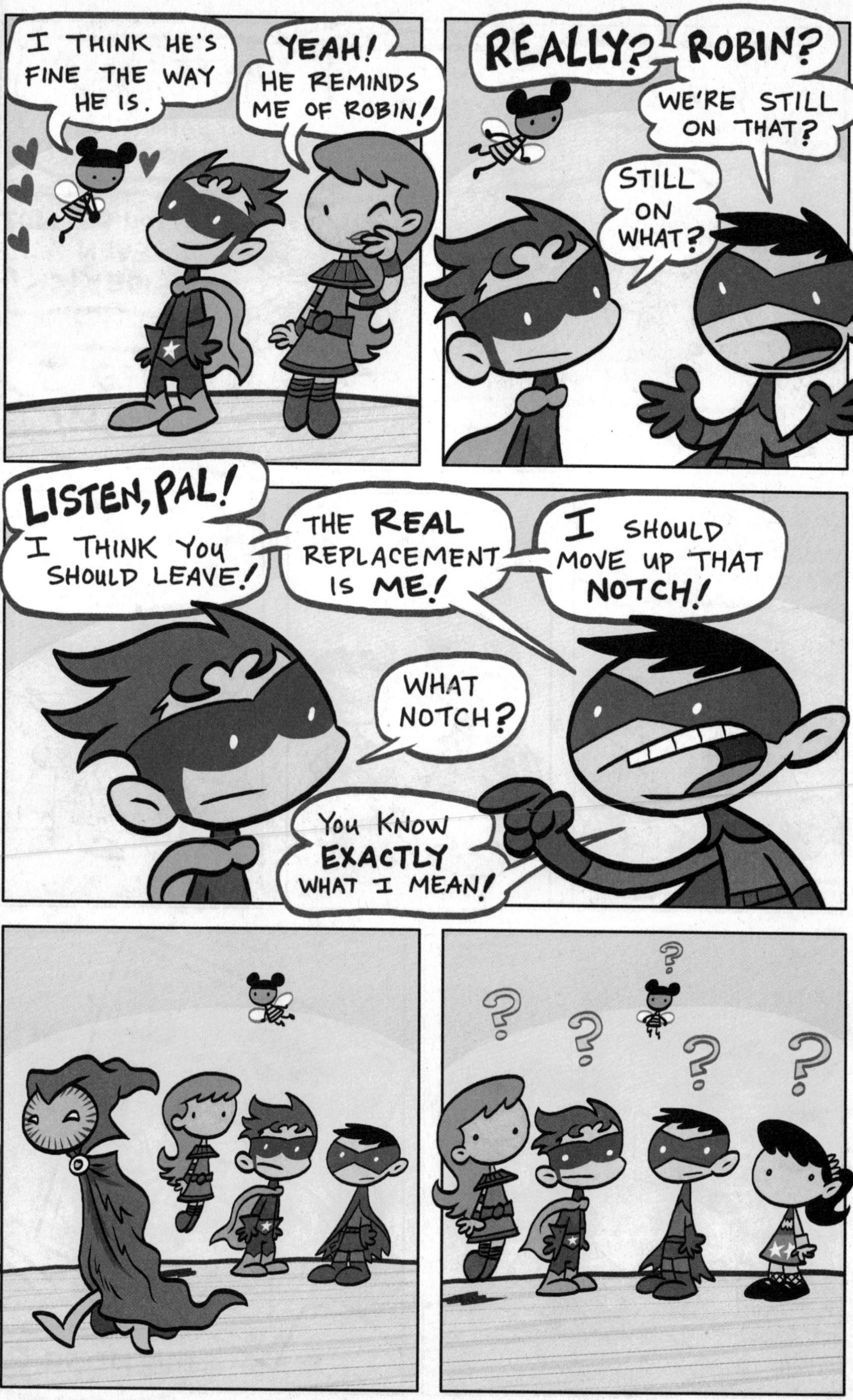
I THINK HE'S FINE THE WAY HE IS.
YEAH! HE REMINDS ME OF ROBIN!
REALLY?
ROBIN?
WE'RE STILL ON THAT?
STILL ON WHAT?
LISTEN, PAL! I THINK YOU SHOULD LEAVE!
THE REAL REPLACEMENT IS ME!
I SHOULD MOVE UP THAT NOTCH!
WHAT NOTCH?
YOU KNOW EXACTLY WHAT I MEAN!

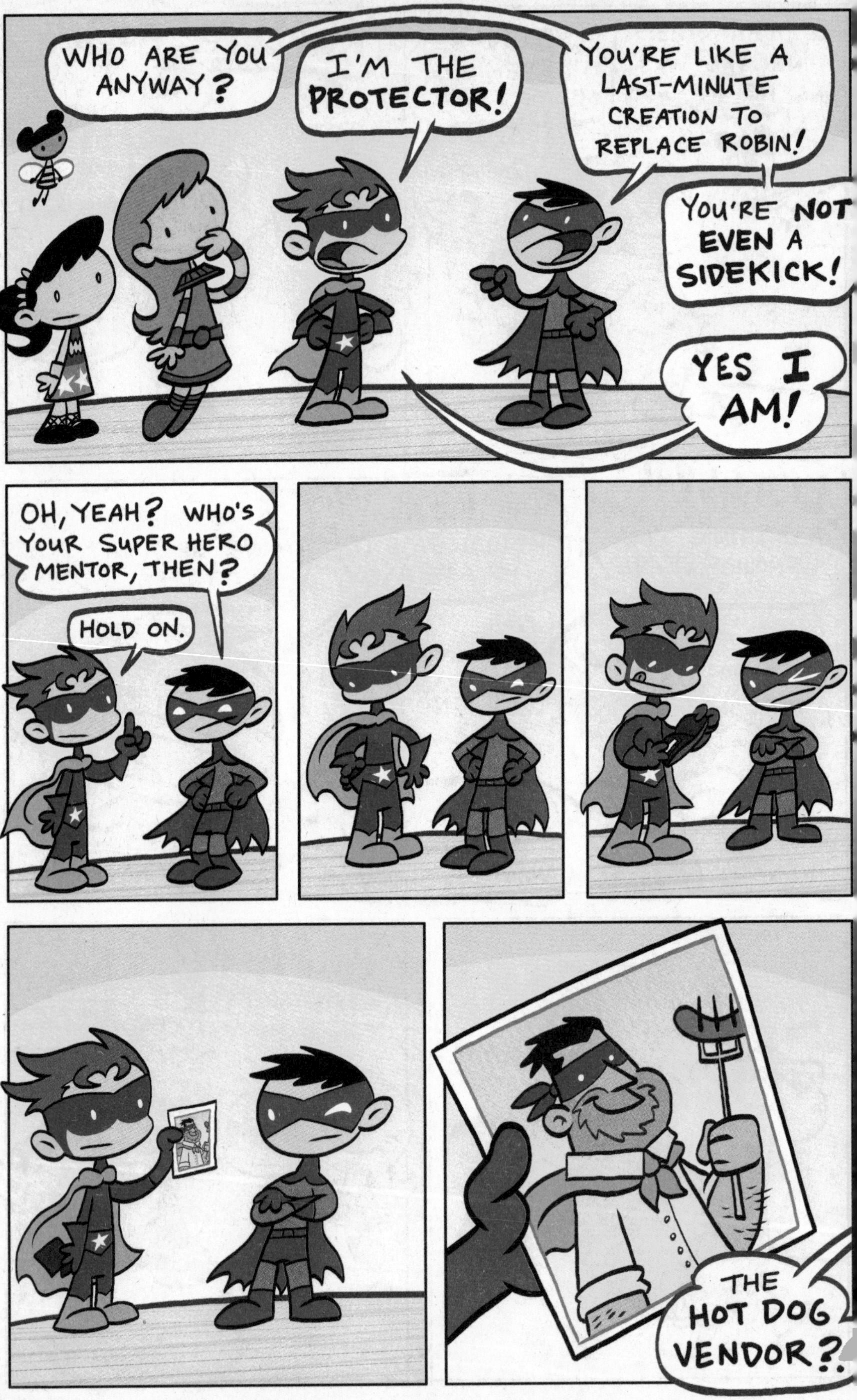

WHO ARE YOU ANYWAY?
I'M THE PROTECTOR!
YOU'RE LIKE A LAST-MINUTE CREATION TO REPLACE ROBIN!
YOU'RE NOT EVEN A SIDEKICK!
YES I AM!
OH, YEAH? WHO'S YOUR SUPER HERO MENTOR, THEN?
HOLD ON.
THE HOT DOG VENDOR?

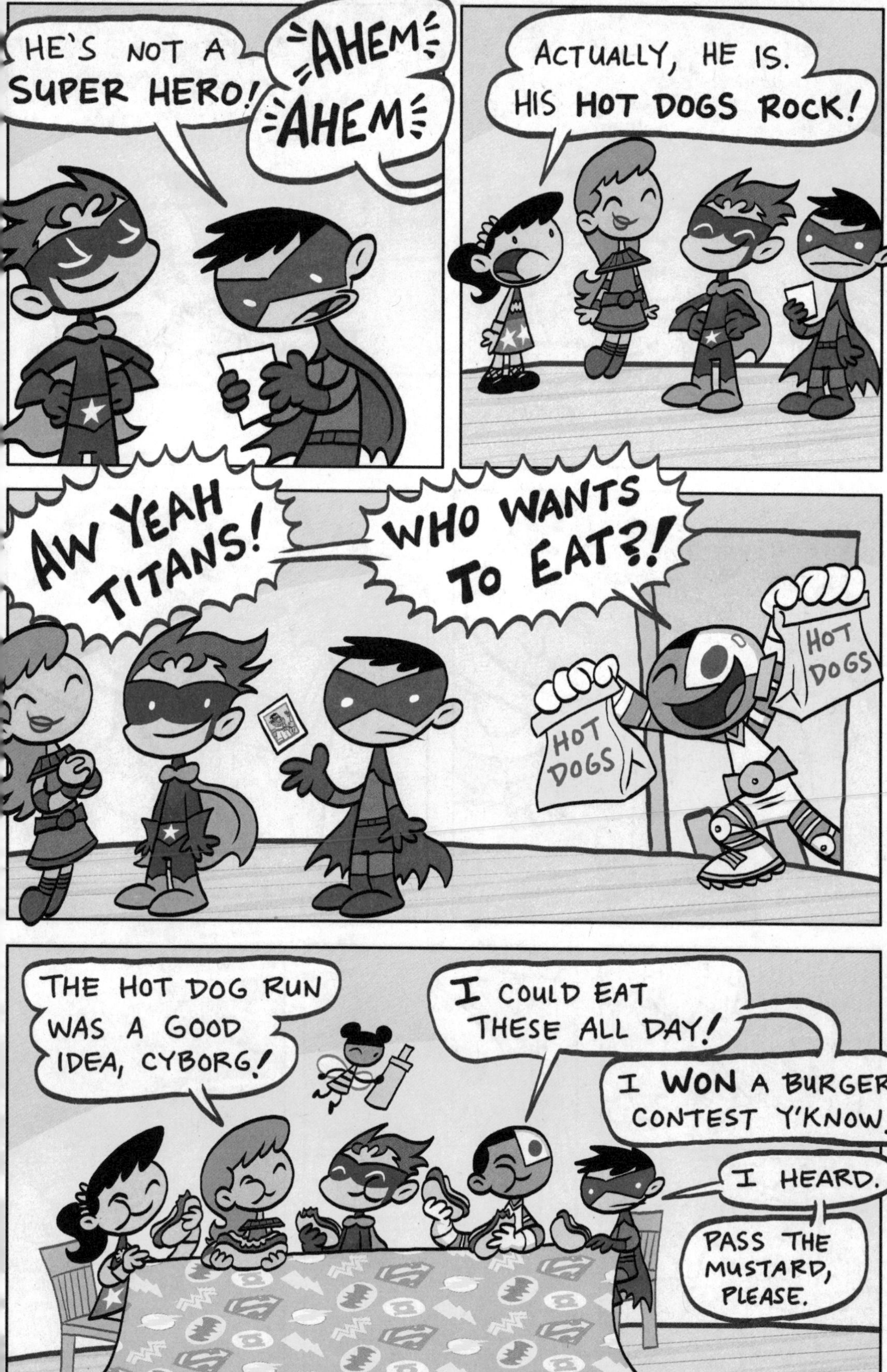
HE'S NOT A SUPER HERO!
AHEM AHEM
ACTUALLY, HE IS. HIS HOT DOGS ROCK!
AW YEAH TITANS!
WHO WANTS TO EAT?!
HOT DOGS
HOT DOGS
THE HOT DOG RUN WAS A GOOD IDEA, CYBORG!
I COULD EAT THESE ALL DAY!
I WON A BURGER CONTEST Y'KNOW!
I HEARD.
PASS THE MUSTARD, PLEASE.

—MENTORLICIOUS.

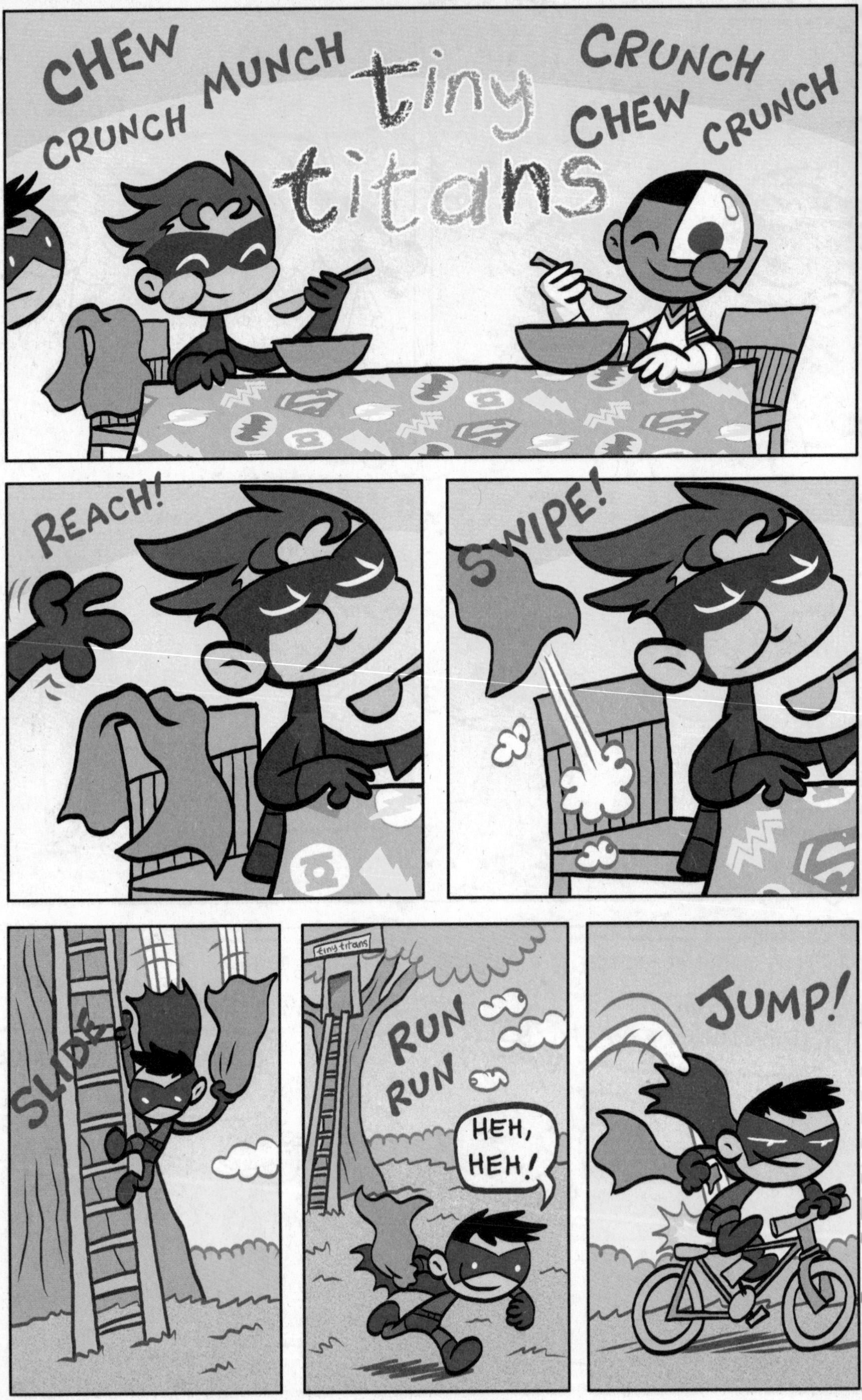
CHEW
CRUNCH
MUNCH
tiny titans
CRUNCH
CHEW
CRUNCH
REACH!
SWIPE!
SLIDE
tiny titans
RUN
RUN
HEH, HEH!
JUMP!

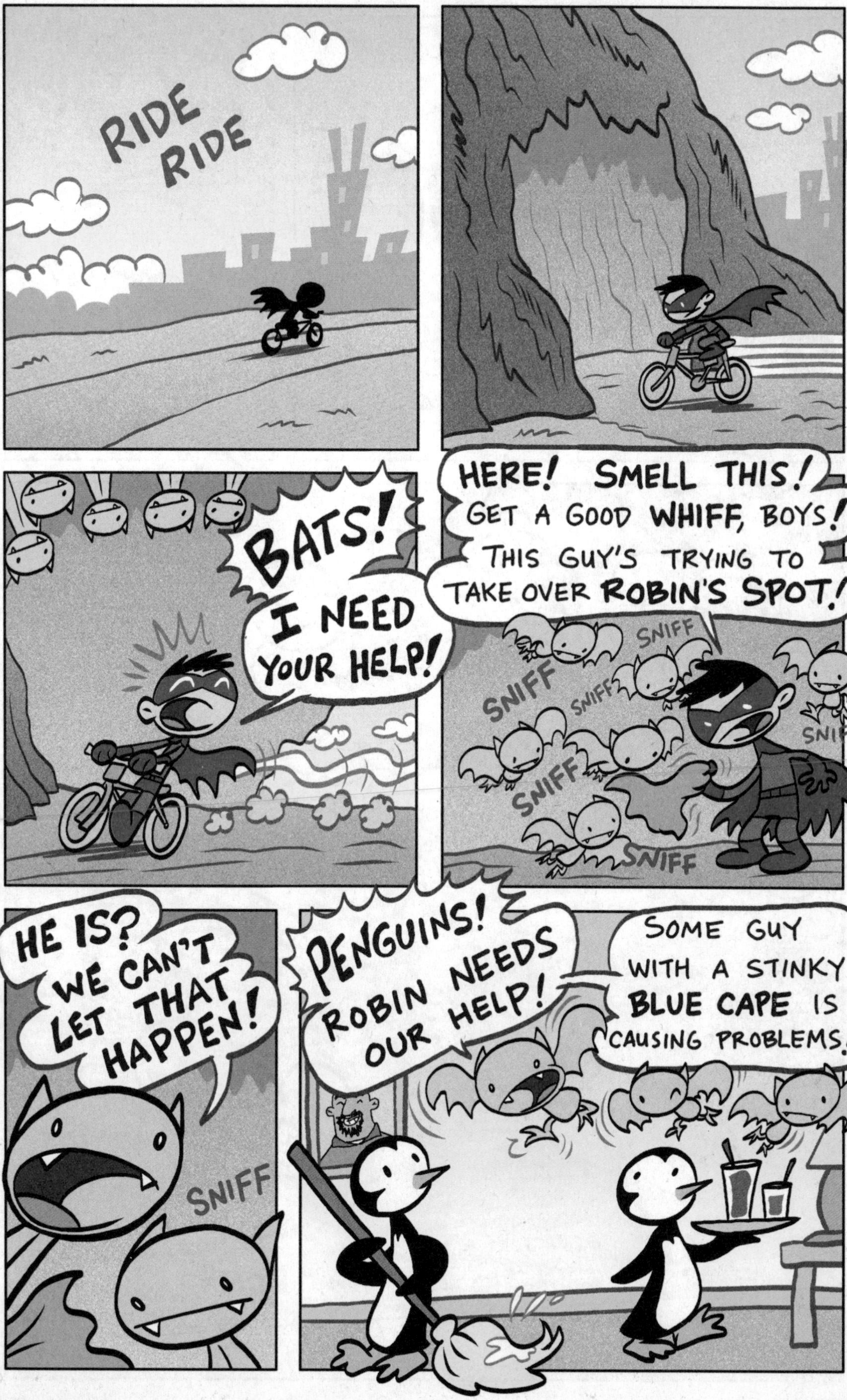

RIDE RIDE
BATS!
I NEED YOUR HELP!
HERE! SMELL THIS! GET A GOOD WHIFF, BOYS! THIS GUY'S TRYING TO TAKE OVER ROBIN'S SPOT!
SNIFF
SNIFF
SNIFF
SNIFF
SNIFF
SNIFF
HE IS? WE CAN'T LET THAT HAPPEN!
SNIFF
PENGUINS! ROBIN NEEDS OUR HELP!
SOME GUY WITH A STINKY BLUE CAPE IS CAUSING PROBLEMS!

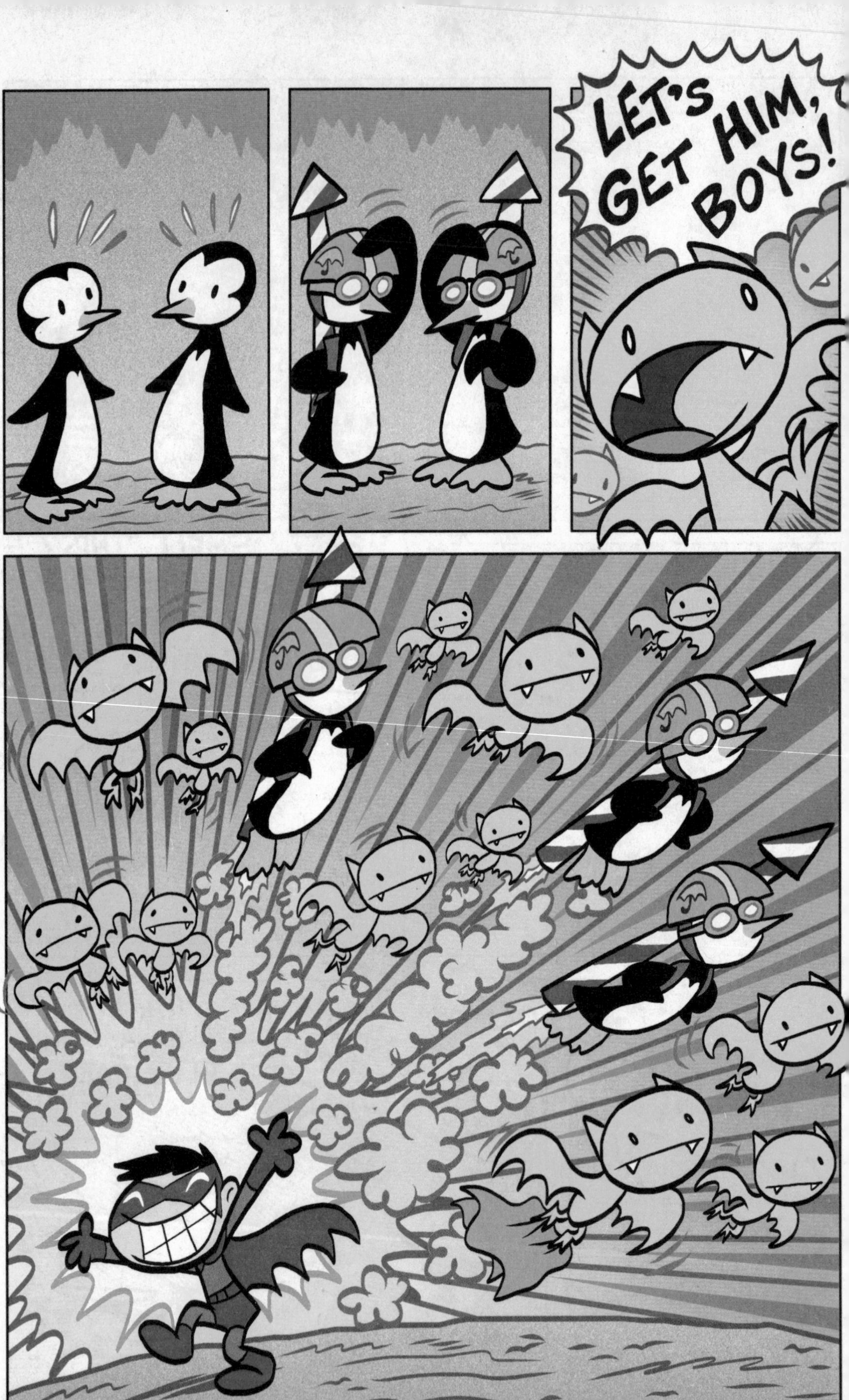
LET'S GET HIM, BOYS!

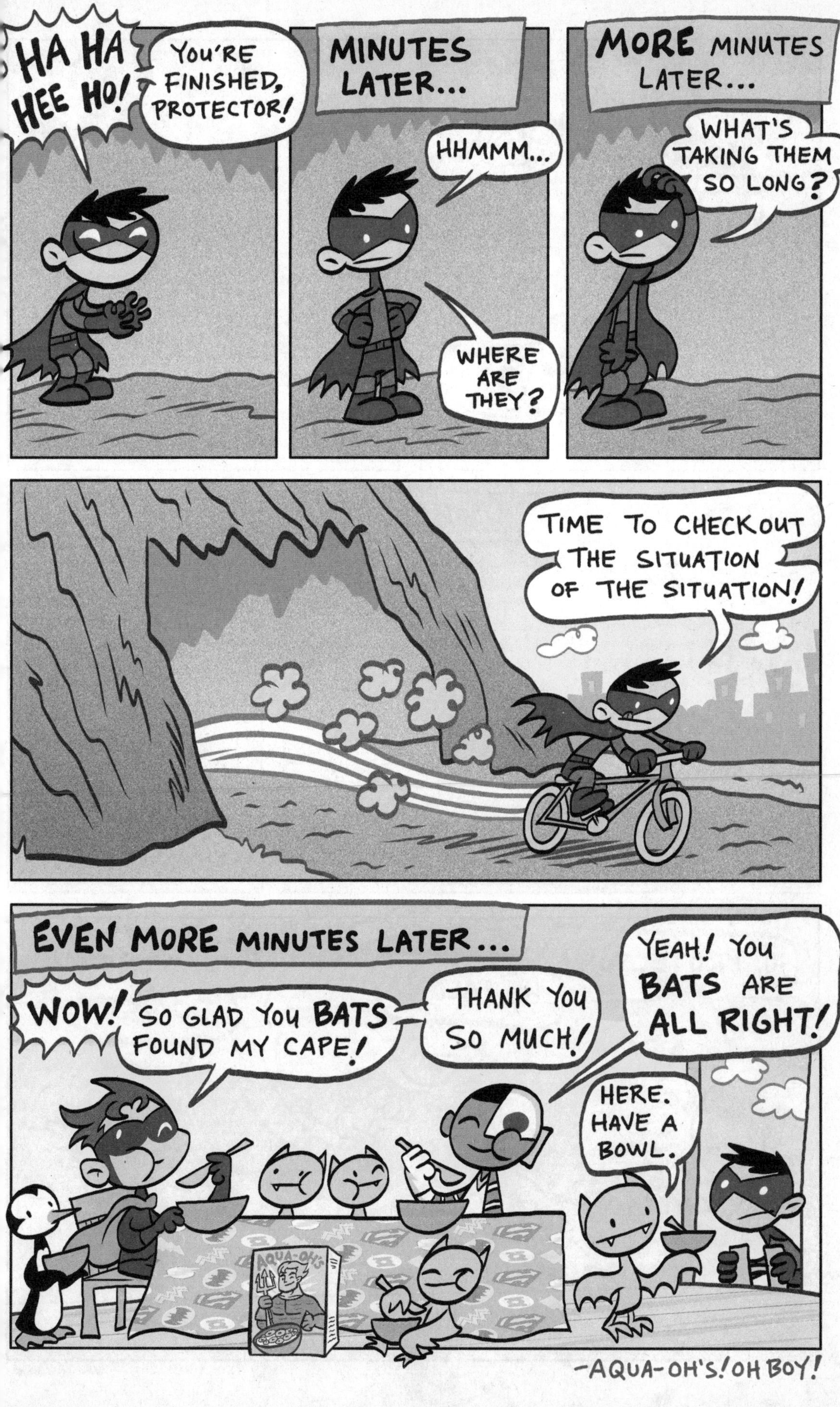
HA HA HEE HO!
YOU'RE FINISHED, PROTECTOR!
MINUTES LATER...
HHMMM...
WHERE ARE THEY?
MORE MINUTES LATER...
WHAT'S TAKING THEM SO LONG?
TIME TO CHECKOUT THE SITUATION OF THE SITUATION!
EVEN MORE MINUTES LATER...
WOW! SO GLAD YOU BATS FOUND MY CAPE!
THANK YOU SO MUCH!
YEAH! YOU BATS ARE ALL RIGHT!
HERE. HAVE A BOWL.
AQUA-OH'S
-AQUA-OH'S! OH BOY!

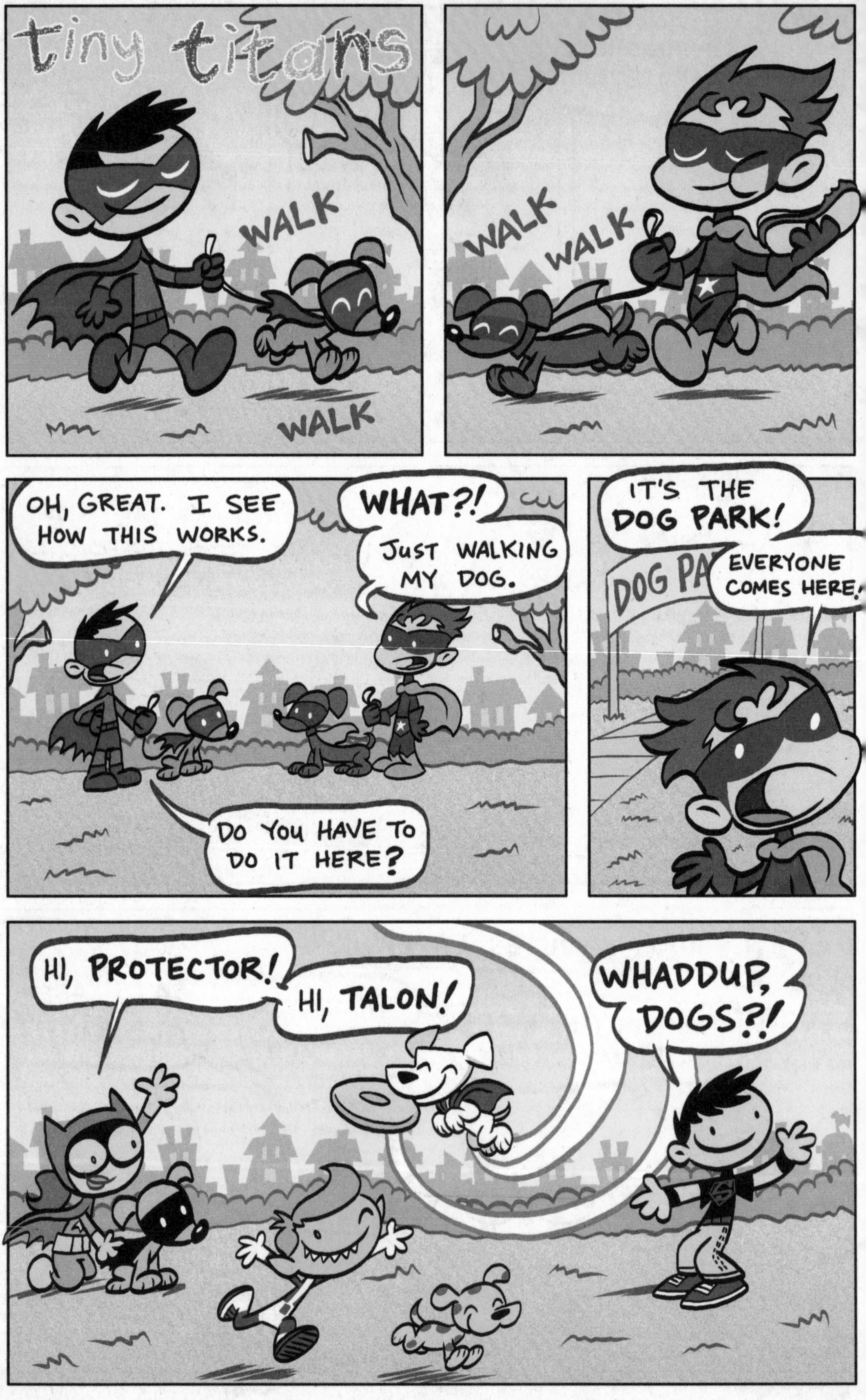
tiny titans
WALK
WALK
WALK
WALK
OH, GREAT. I SEE HOW THIS WORKS.
WHAT?!
JUST WALKING MY DOG.
DO YOU HAVE TO DO IT HERE?
IT'S THE DOG PARK!
DOG PA
EVERYONE COMES HERE.
HI, PROTECTOR!
HI, TALON!
WHADDUP, DOGS?!

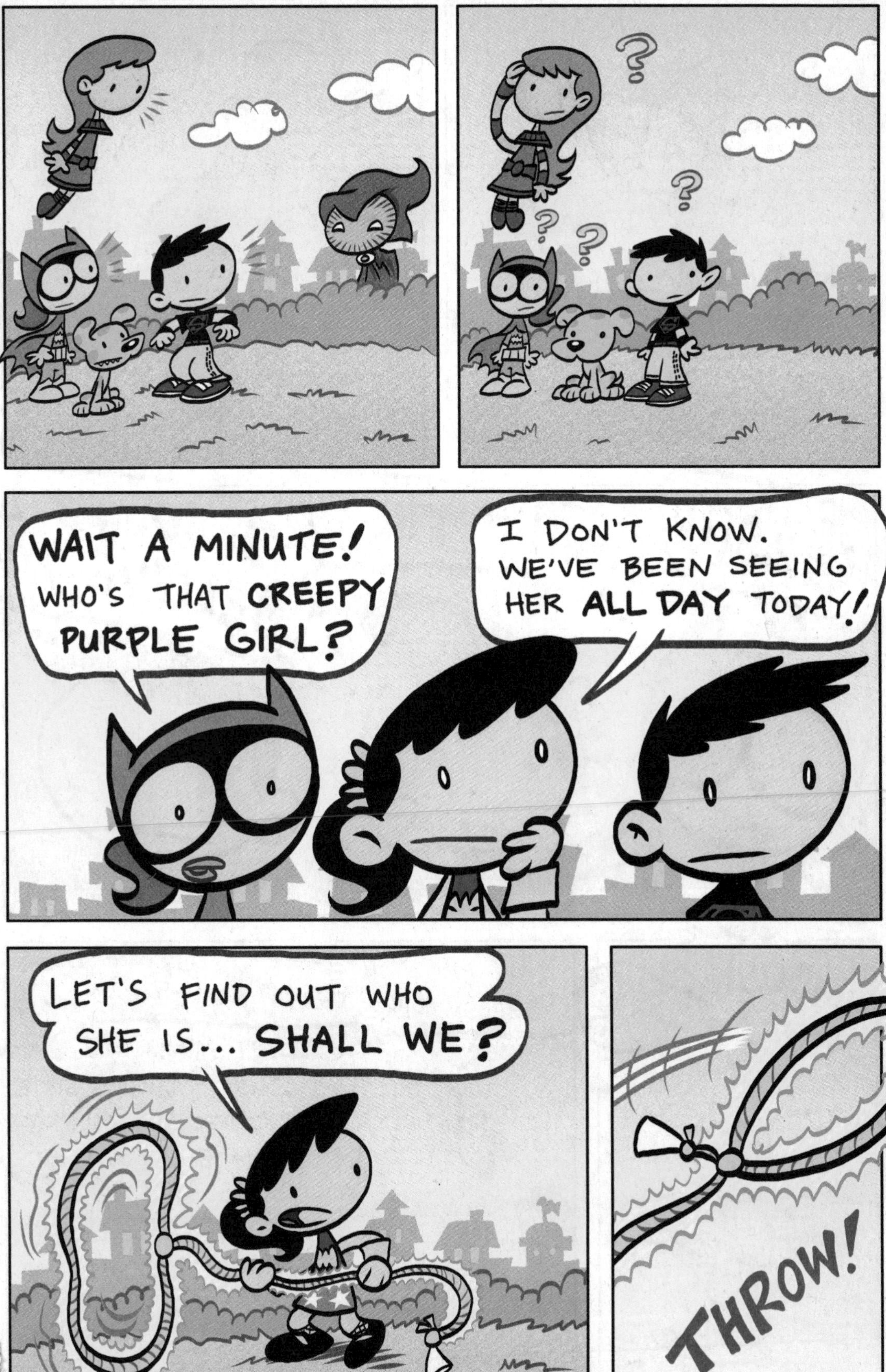
WAIT A MINUTE! WHO'S THAT CREEPY PURPLE GIRL?
I DON'T KNOW. WE'VE BEEN SEEING HER ALL DAY TODAY!
LET'S FIND OUT WHO SHE IS... SHALL WE?
THROW!

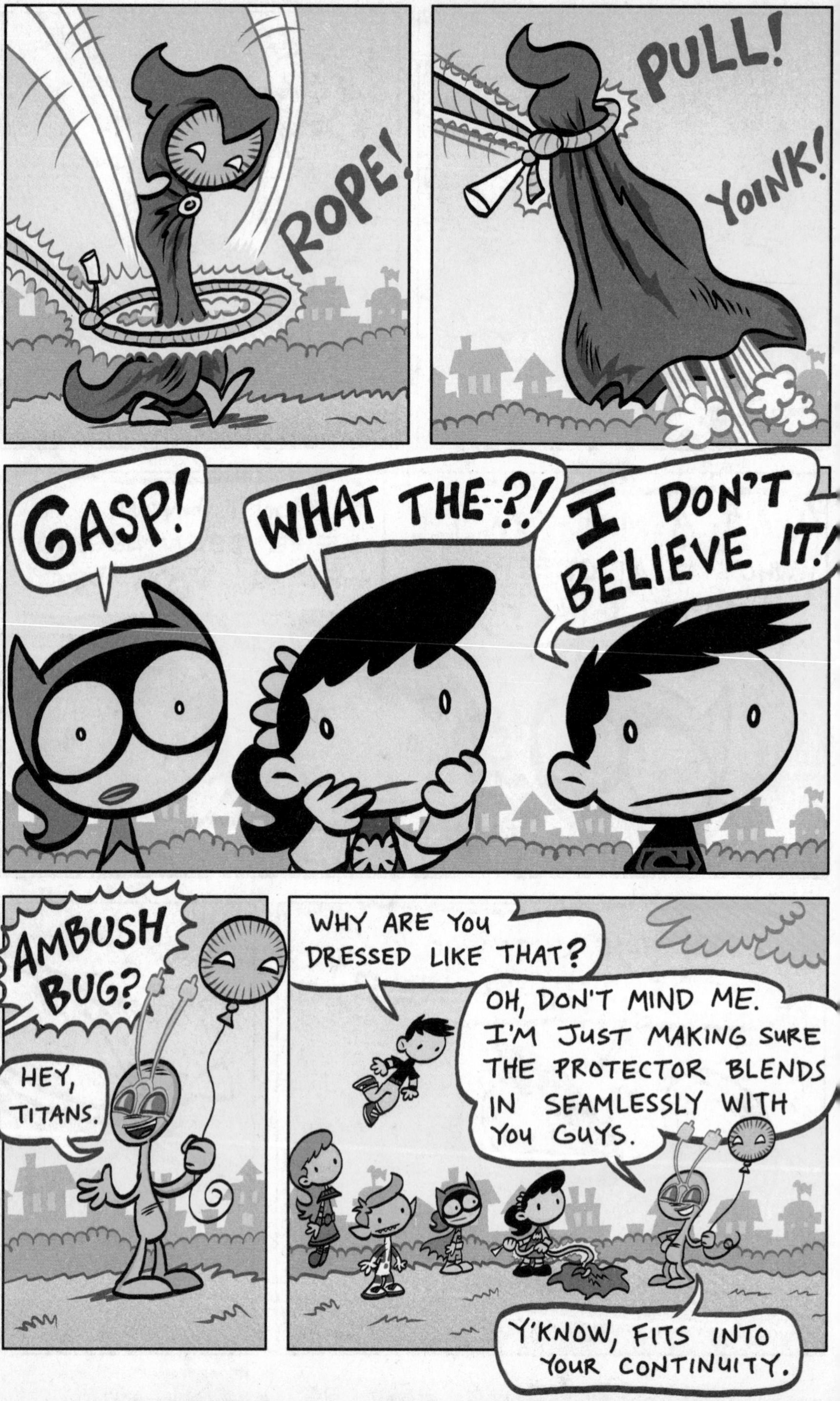

ROPE!
PULL!
YOINK!
GASP!
WHAT THE--?!
I DON'T BELIEVE IT!
AMBUSH BUG?
HEY, TITANS.
WHY ARE YOU DRESSED LIKE THAT?
OH, DON'T MIND ME. I'M JUST MAKING SURE THE PROTECTOR BLENDS IN SEAMLESSLY WITH YOU GUYS.
Y'KNOW, FITS INTO YOUR CONTINUITY.

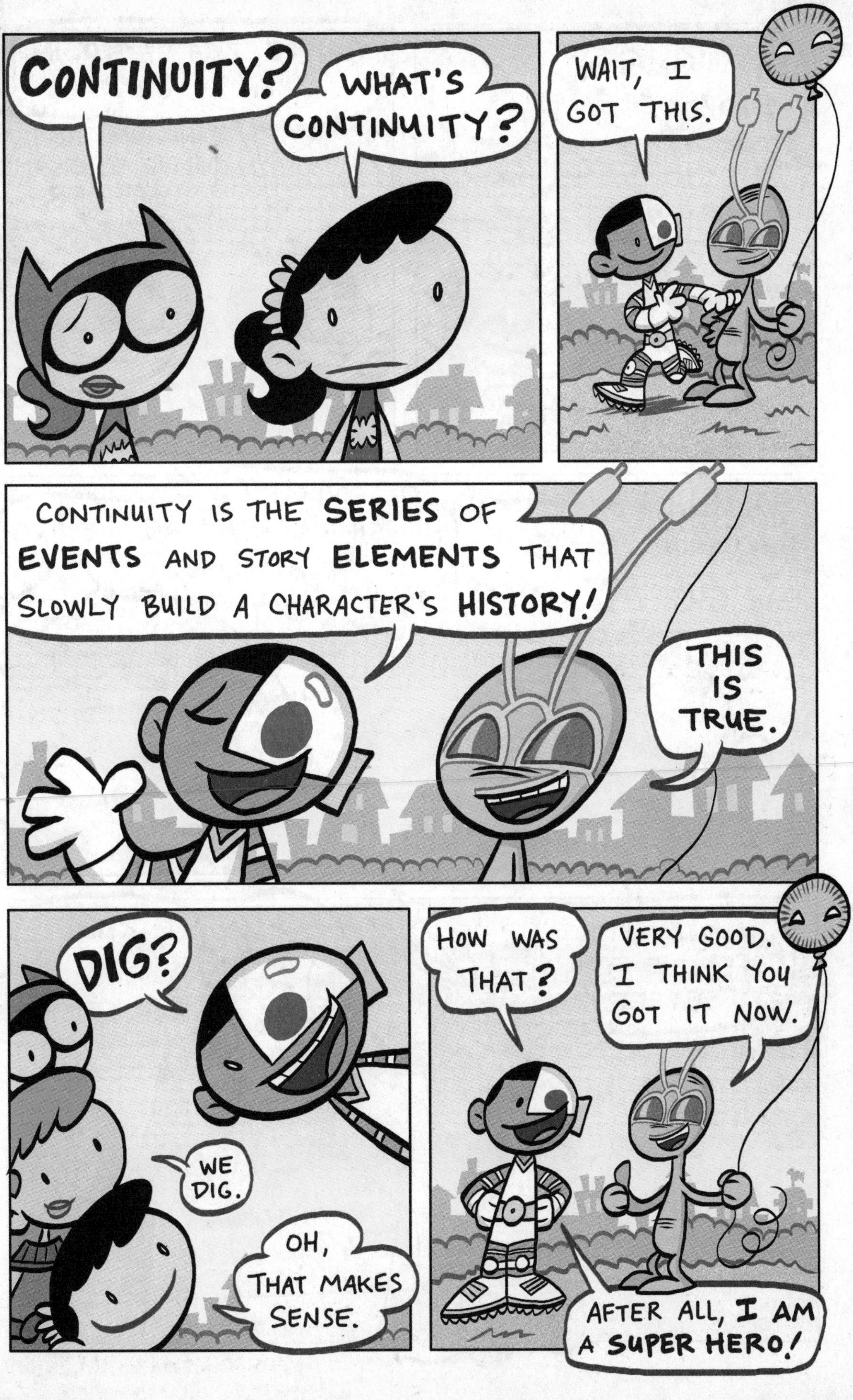
CONTINUITY?
WHAT'S CONTINUITY?
WAIT, I GOT THIS.
CONTINUITY IS THE SERIES OF EVENTS AND STORY ELEMENTS THAT SLOWLY BUILD A CHARACTER'S HISTORY!
THIS IS TRUE.
DIG?
WE DIG.
OH, THAT MAKES SENSE.
HOW WAS THAT?
VERY GOOD. I THINK YOU GOT IT NOW.
AFTER ALL, I AM A SUPER HERO!

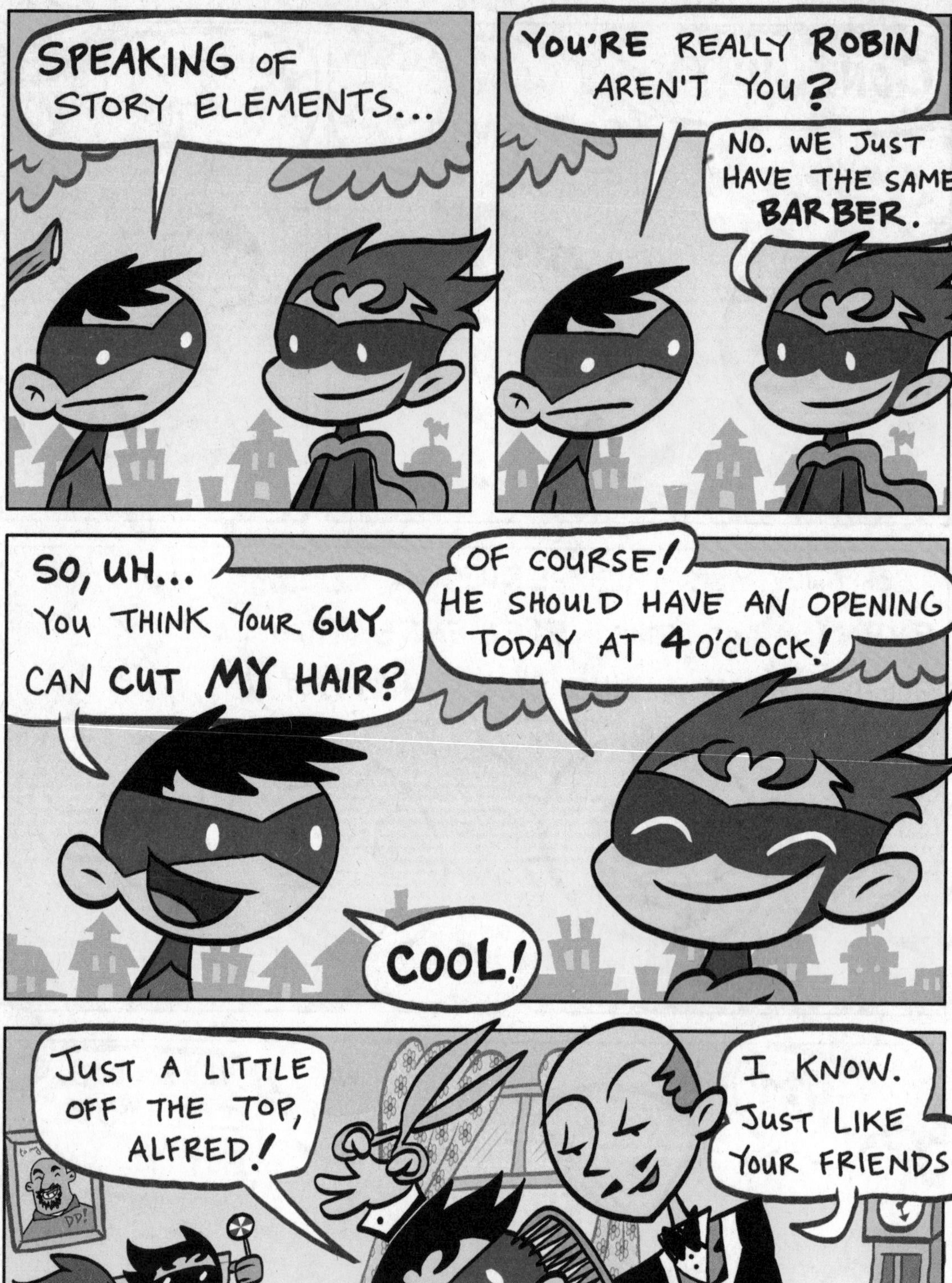
SPEAKING OF STORY ELEMENTS...
YOU'RE REALLY ROBIN AREN'T YOU?
NO. WE JUST HAVE THE SAME BARBER.
SO, UH... YOU THINK YOUR GUY CAN CUT MY HAIR?
OF COURSE! HE SHOULD HAVE AN OPENING TODAY AT 4 O'CLOCK!
COOL!
JUST A LITTLE OFF THE TOP, ALFRED!
I KNOW. JUST LIKE YOUR FRIENDS.

—THAT'S THE WAY...UH, HUH!

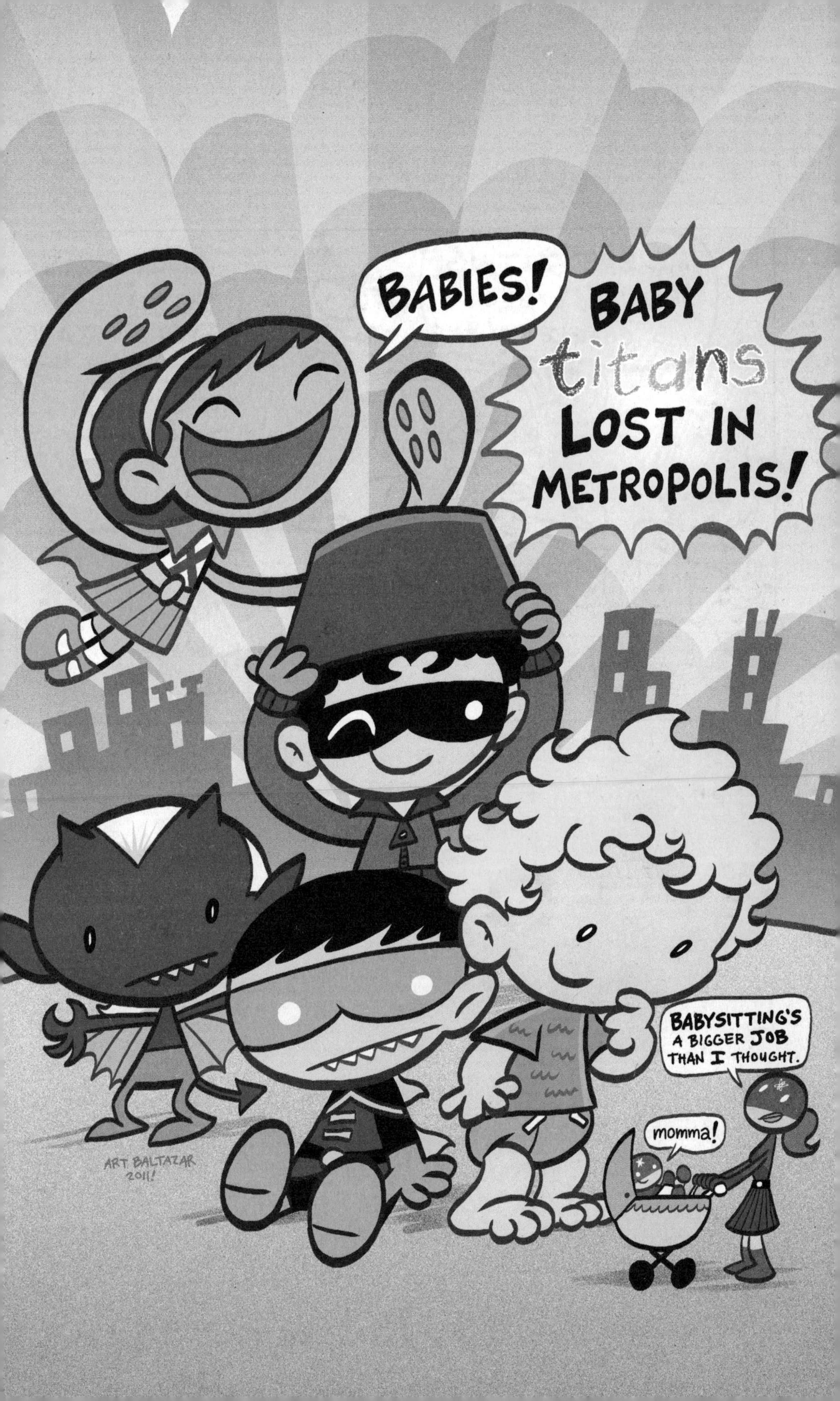
BABIES!
BABY titans LOST IN METROPOLIS!
BABYSITTING'S A BIGGER JOB THAN I THOUGHT.
momma!
ART BALTAZAR 2011!

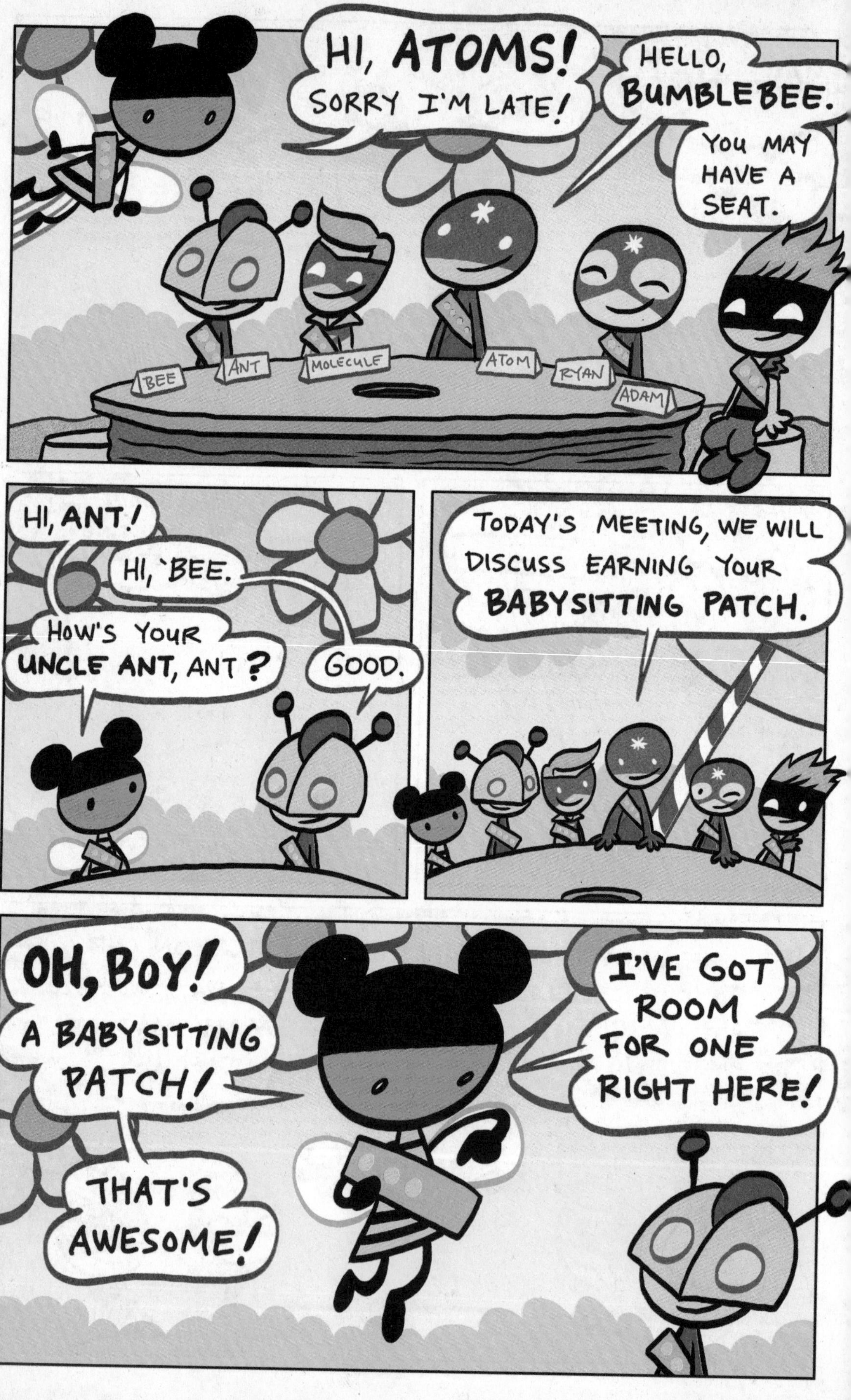

HI, ATOMS! SORRY I'M LATE!
HELLO, BUMBLEBEE.
YOU MAY HAVE A SEAT.
BEE
ANT
MOLECULE
ATOM
RYAN
ADAM
HI, ANT!
HI, `BEE.
HOW'S YOUR UNCLE ANT, ANT?
GOOD.
TODAY'S MEETING, WE WILL DISCUSS EARNING YOUR BABYSITTING PATCH.
OH, BOY! A BABYSITTING PATCH!
THAT'S AWESOME!
I'VE GOT ROOM FOR ONE RIGHT HERE!

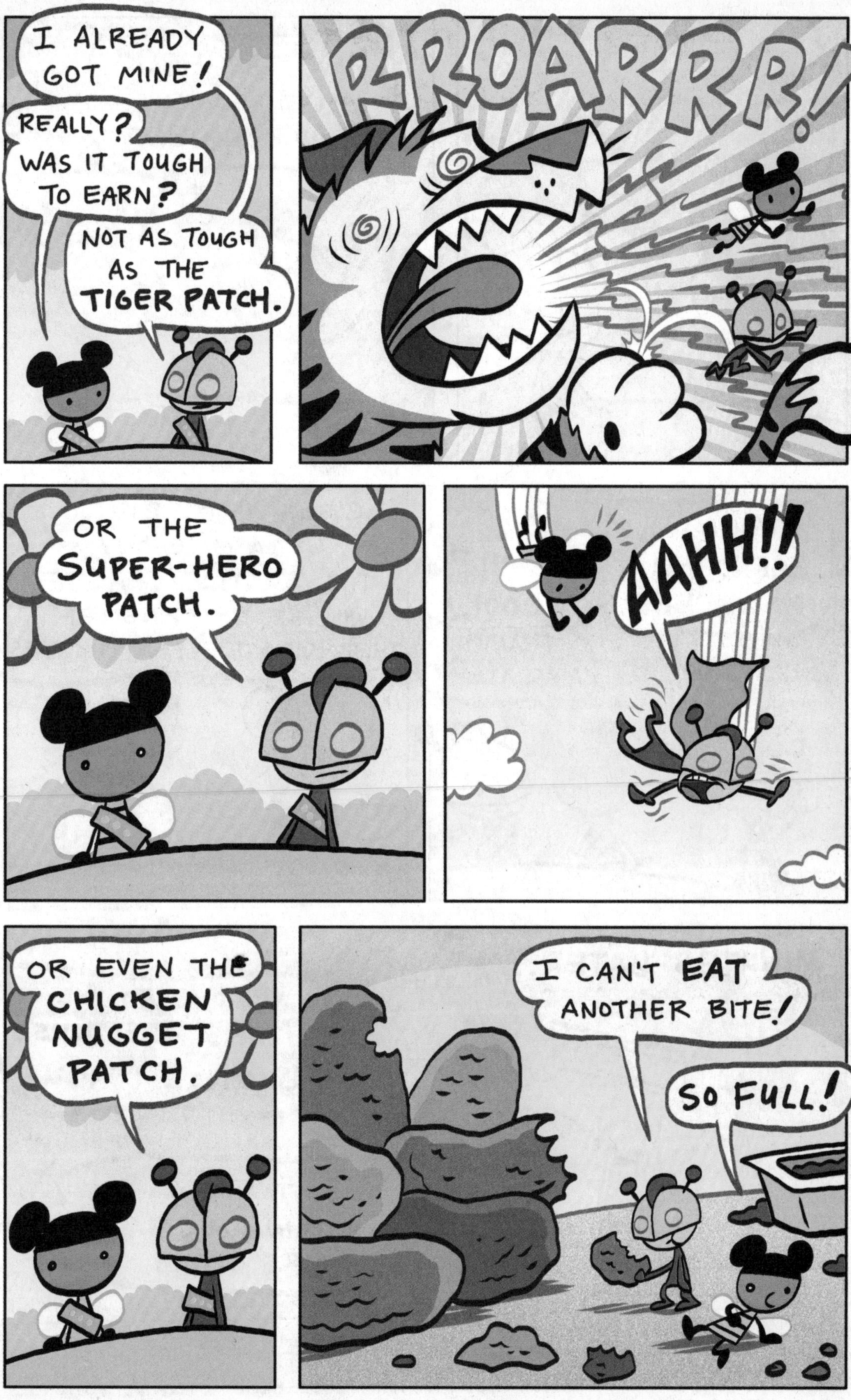
I ALREADY GOT MINE!
REALLY? WAS IT TOUGH TO EARN?
NOT AS TOUGH AS THE TIGER PATCH.
RROARRR!
OR THE SUPER-HERO PATCH.
AAHH!!
OR EVEN THE CHICKEN NUGGET PATCH.
I CAN'T EAT ANOTHER BITE!
SO FULL!

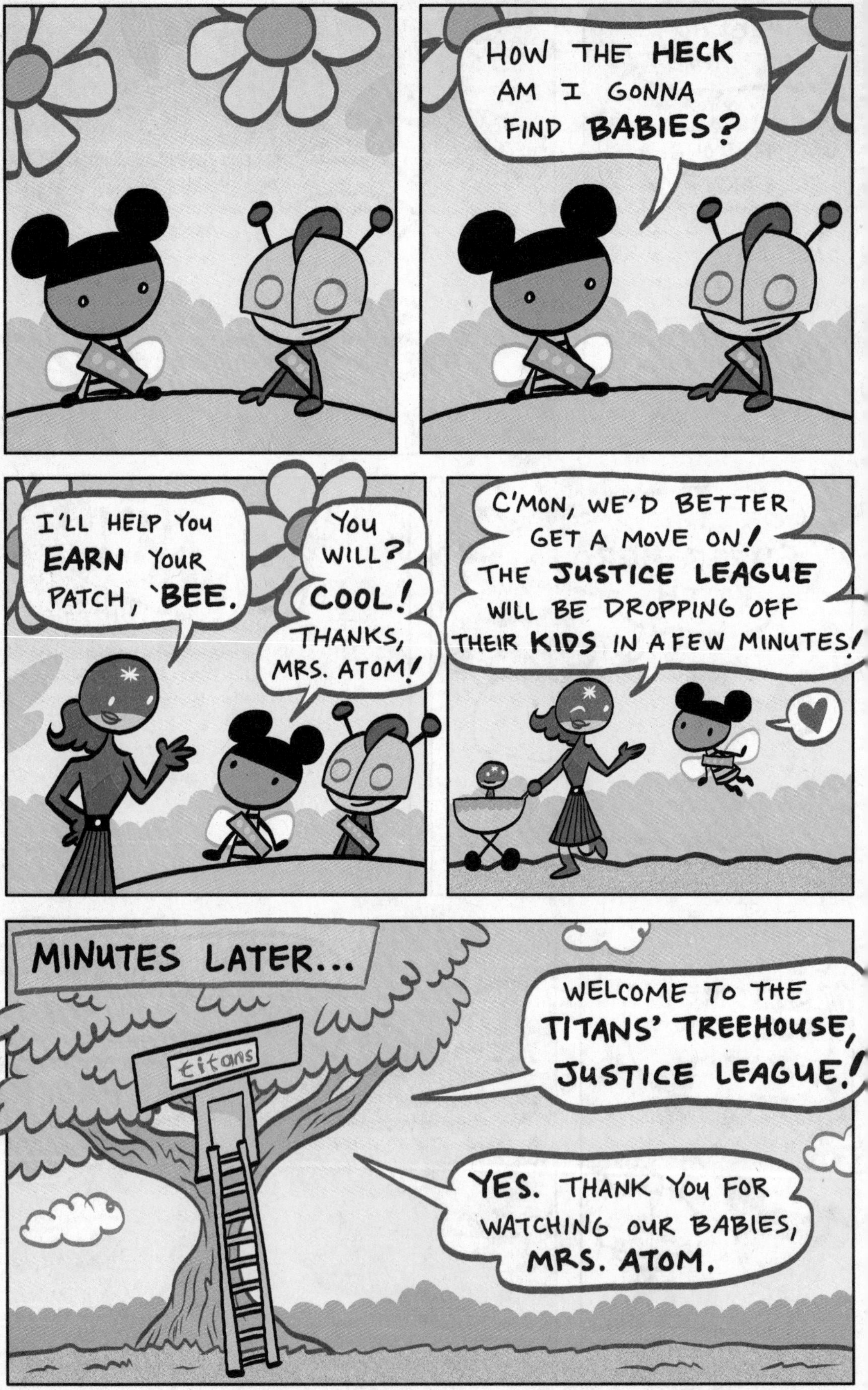

HOW THE HECK AM I GONNA FIND BABIES?
I'LL HELP YOU EARN YOUR PATCH, 'BEE.
YOU WILL? COOL! THANKS, MRS. ATOM!
C'MON, WE'D BETTER GET A MOVE ON! THE JUSTICE LEAGUE WILL BE DROPPING OFF THEIR KIDS IN A FEW MINUTES!
MINUTES LATER...
titans
WELCOME TO THE TITANS' TREEHOUSE, JUSTICE LEAGUE!
YES. THANK YOU FOR WATCHING OUR BABIES, MRS. ATOM.

-EARN THAT PATCH!

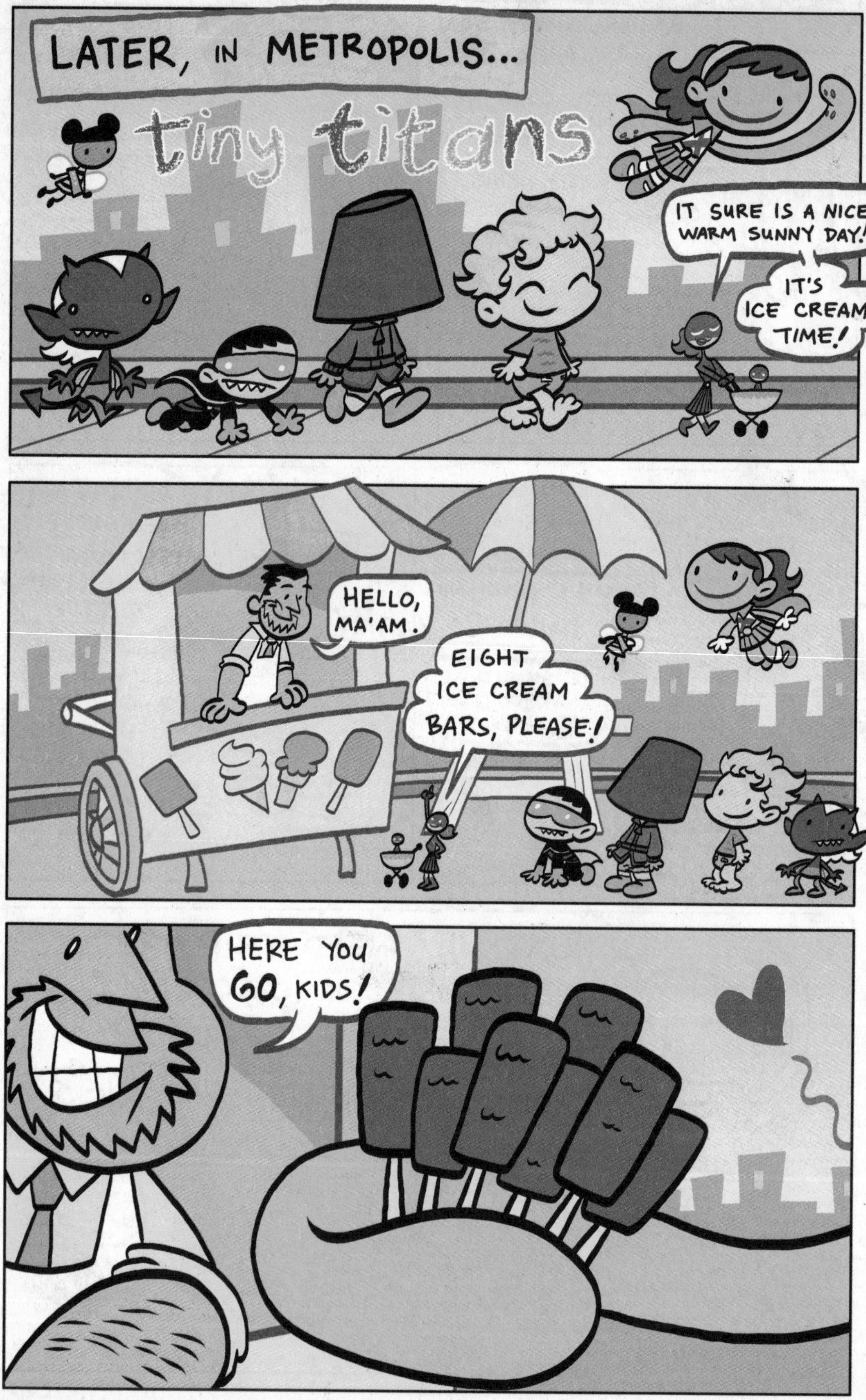
LATER, IN METROPOLIS...
tiny titans
IT SURE IS A NICE WARM SUNNY DAY!
IT'S ICE CREAM TIME!
HELLO, MA'AM.
EIGHT ICE CREAM BARS, PLEASE!
HERE YOU GO, KIDS!

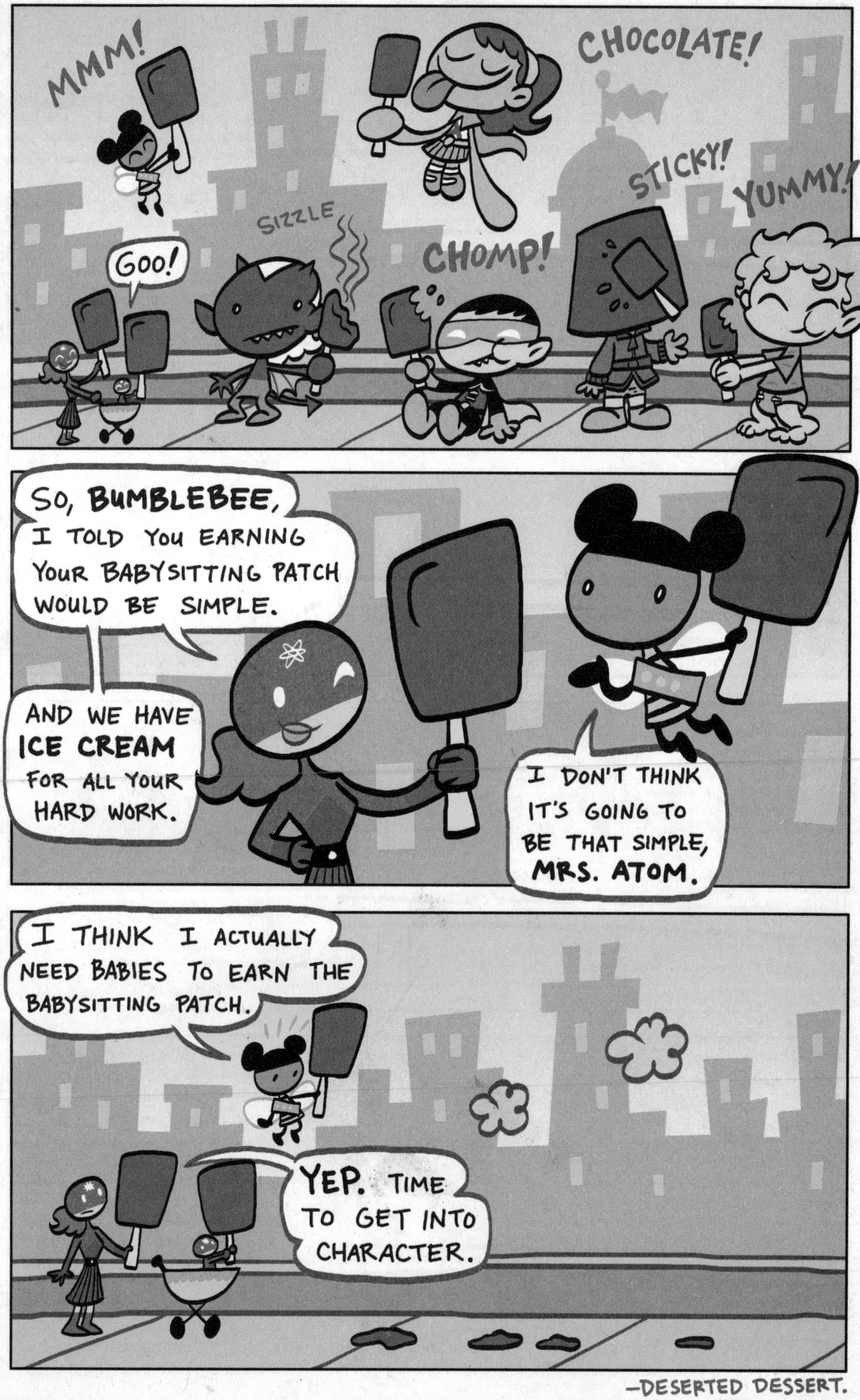

MMM!
CHOCOLATE!
STICKY!
YUMMY!
SIZZLE
GOO!
CHOMP!
So, BUMBLEBEE, I TOLD YOU EARNING YOUR BABYSITTING PATCH WOULD BE SIMPLE.
AND WE HAVE ICE CREAM FOR ALL YOUR HARD WORK.
I DON'T THINK IT'S GOING TO BE THAT SIMPLE, MRS. ATOM.
I THINK I ACTUALLY NEED BABIES TO EARN THE BABYSITTING PATCH.
YEP. TIME TO GET INTO CHARACTER.

–DESERTED DESSERT.

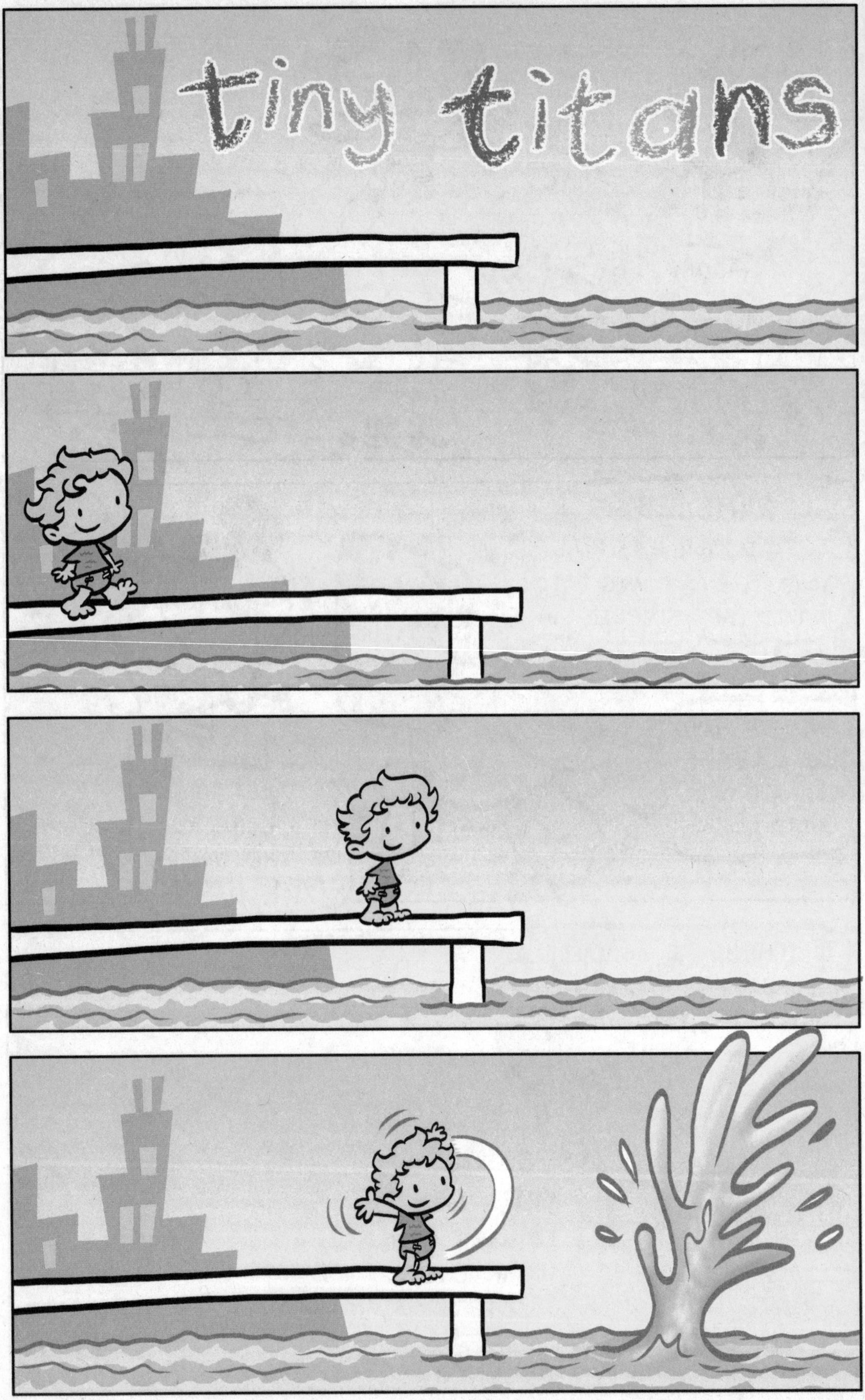
tiny titans

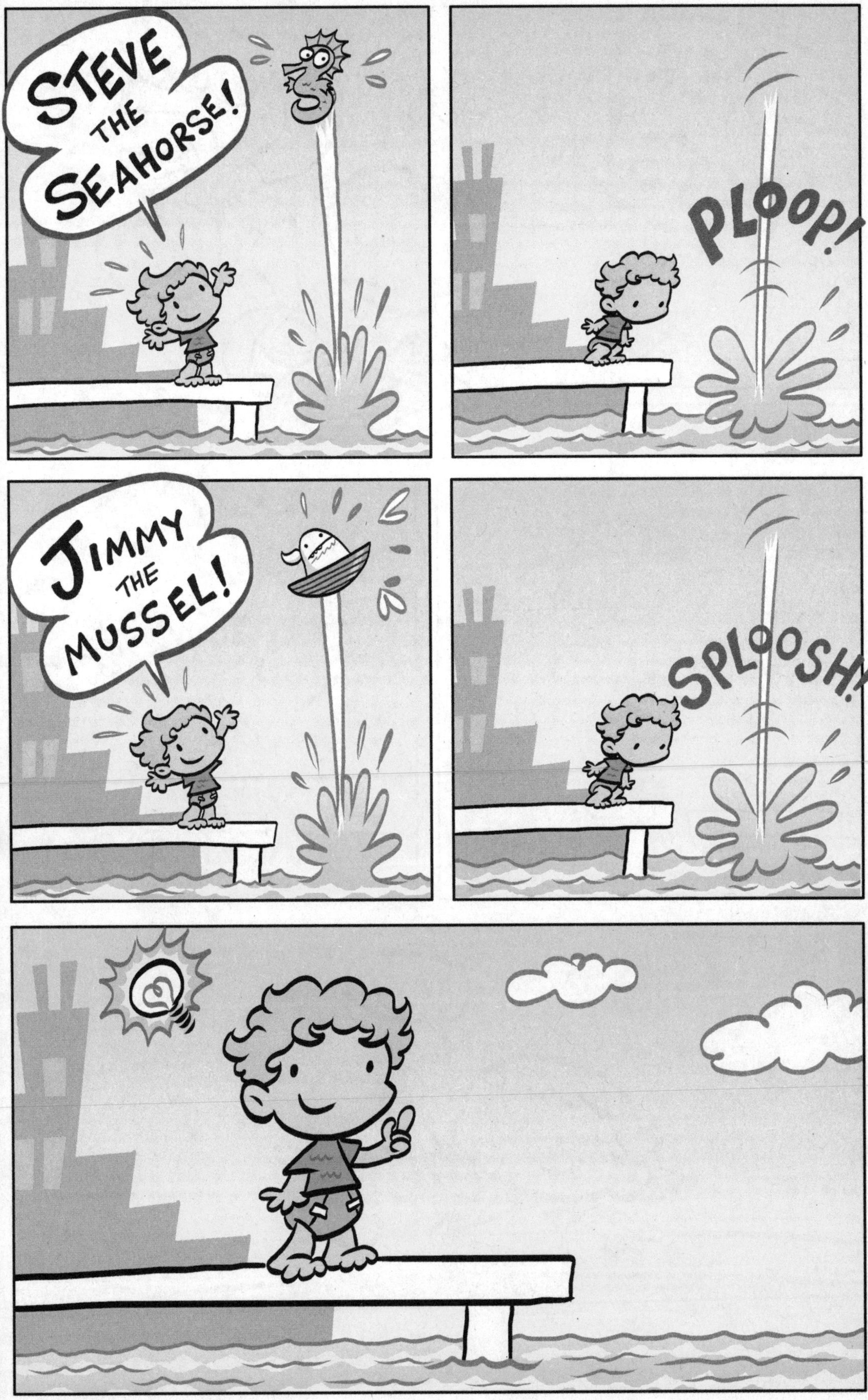
STEVE THE SEAHORSE!
PLOOP!
JIMMY THE MUSSEL!
SPLOOSH!

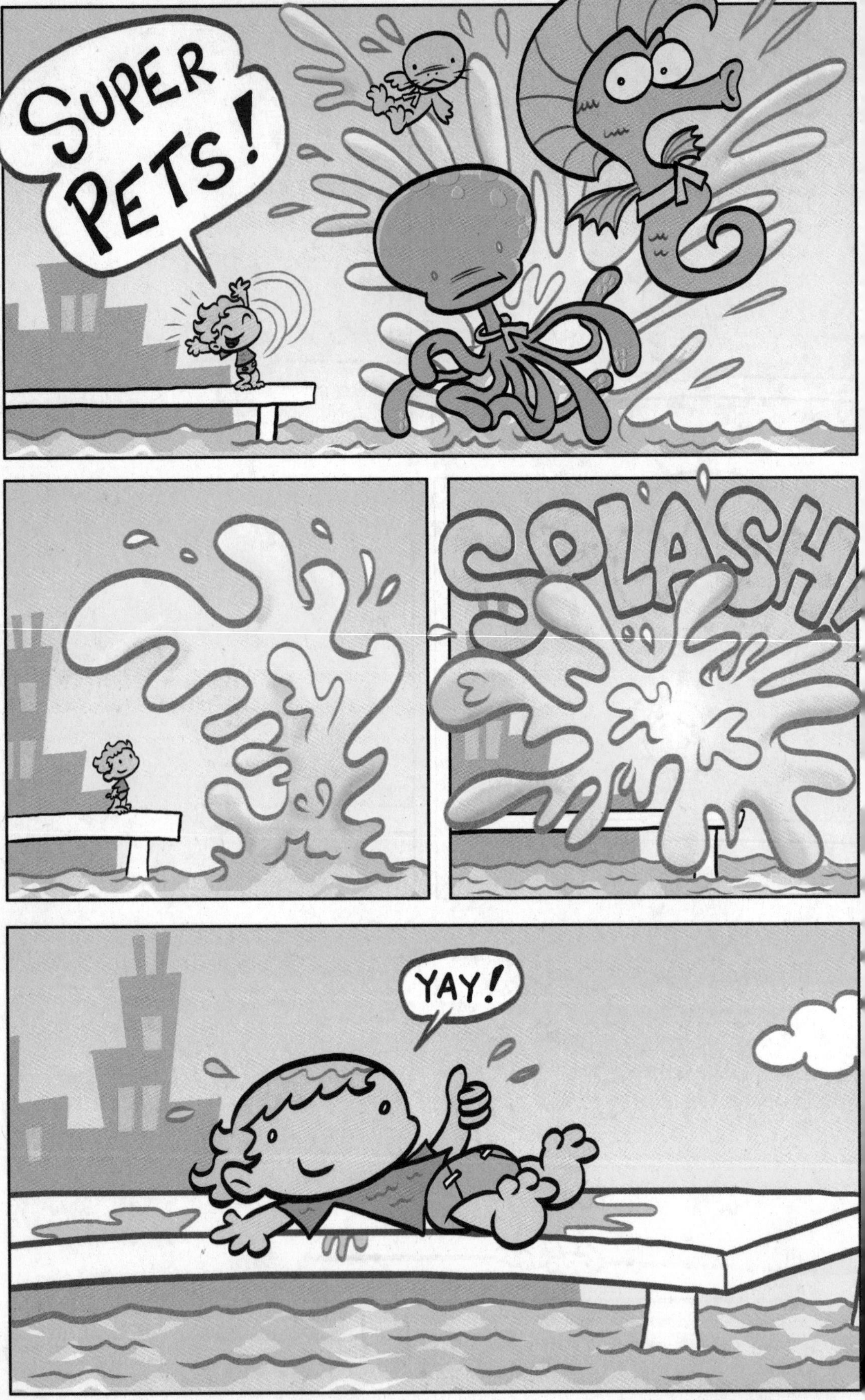

SUPER PETS!
SPLASH!
YAY!

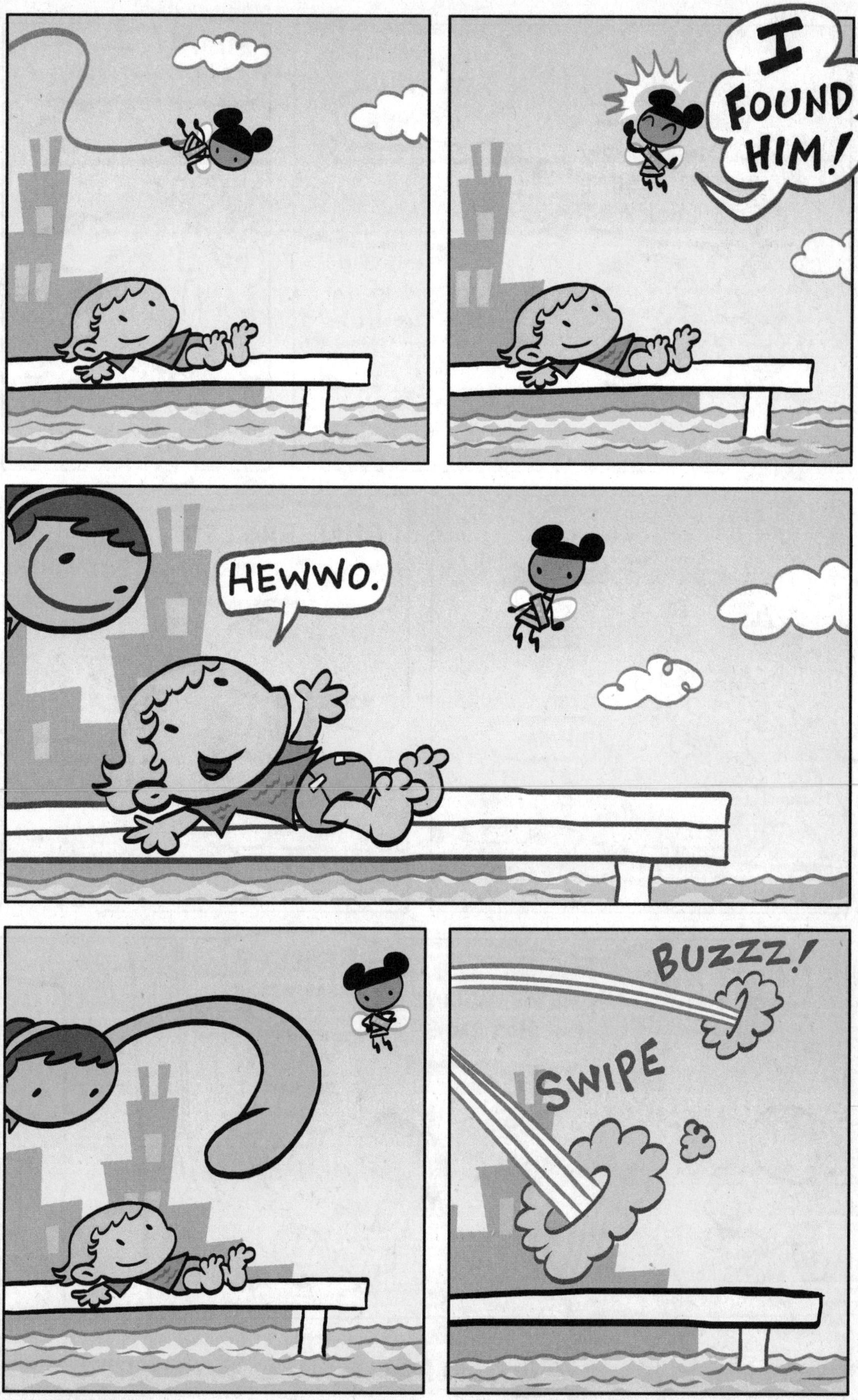
I FOUND HIM!
HEWWO.
BUZZZ!
SWIPE

—WATER.

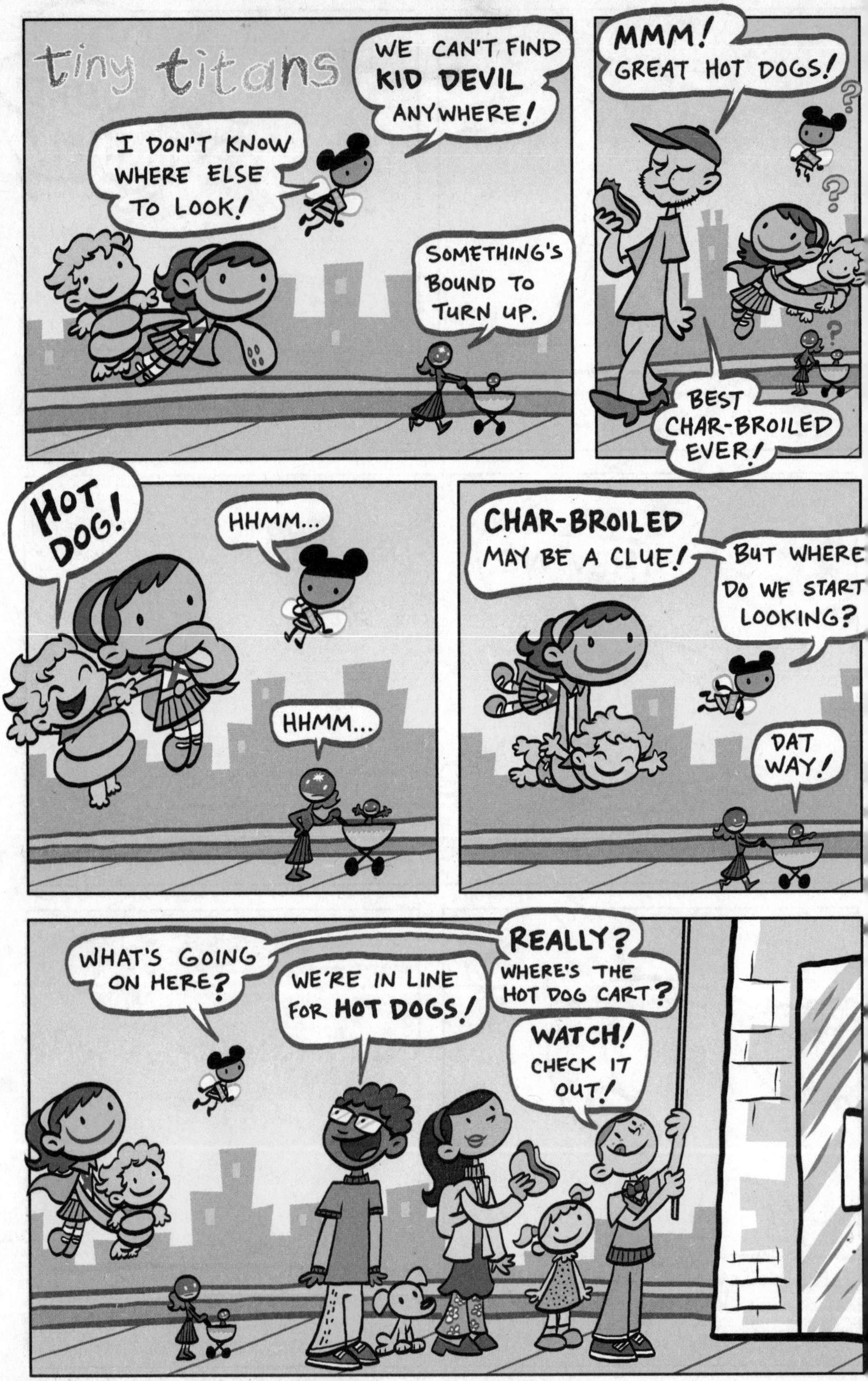
tiny titans
WE CAN'T FIND KID DEVIL ANYWHERE!
I DON'T KNOW WHERE ELSE TO LOOK!
SOMETHING'S BOUND TO TURN UP.
MMM! GREAT HOT DOGS!
BEST CHAR-BROILED EVER!
?
?
?
HOT DOG!
HHMM...
HHMM...
CHAR-BROILED MAY BE A CLUE!
BUT WHERE DO WE START LOOKING?
DAT WAY!
WHAT'S GOING ON HERE?
WE'RE IN LINE FOR HOT DOGS!
REALLY? WHERE'S THE HOT DOG CART?
WATCH! CHECK IT OUT!

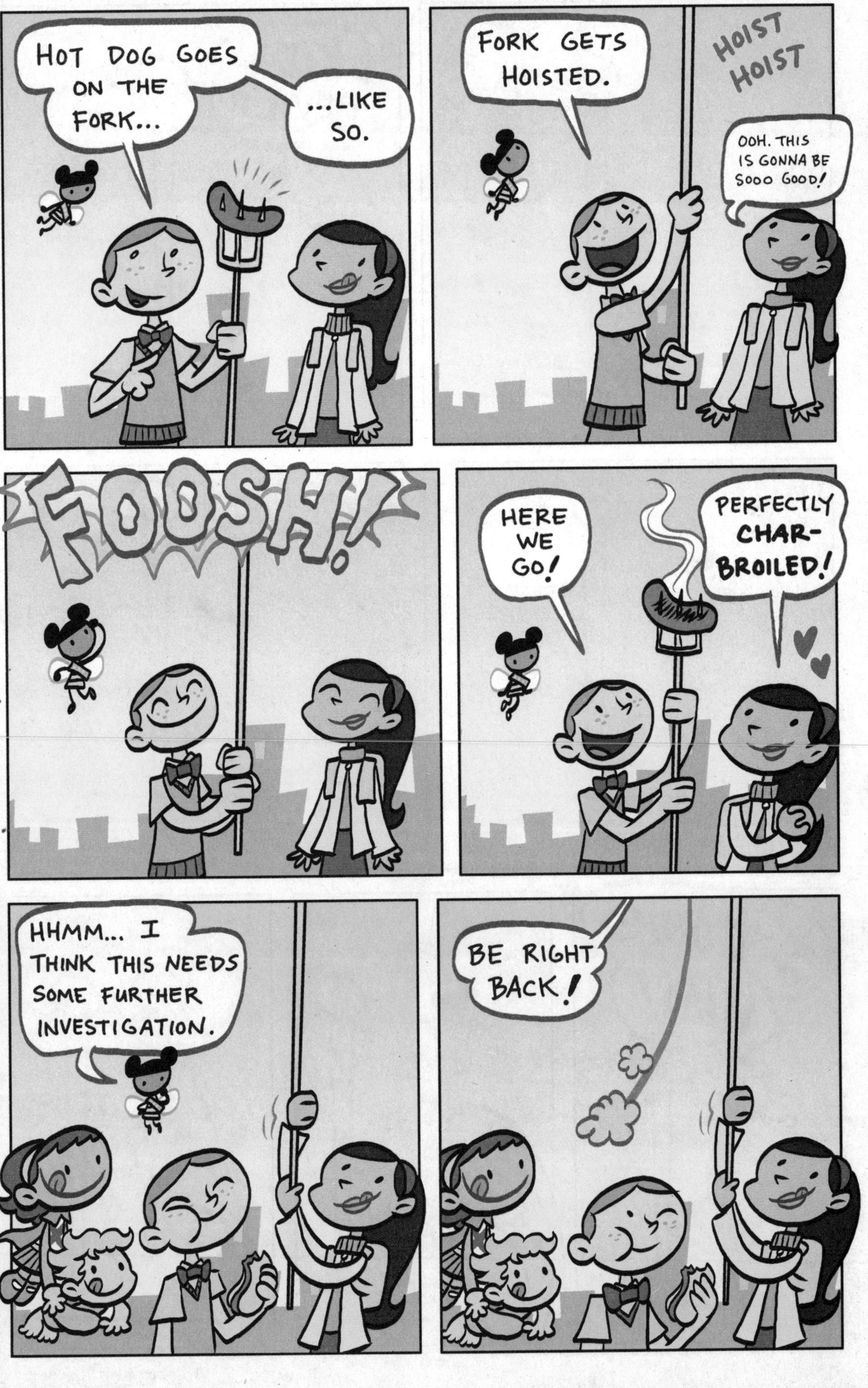
HOT DOG GOES ON THE FORK...
...LIKE SO.
FORK GETS HOISTED.
HOIST HOIST
OOH. THIS IS GONNA BE SOOO GOOD!
FOOSH!
HERE WE GO!
PERFECTLY CHAR-BROILED!
HHMM... I THINK THIS NEEDS SOME FURTHER INVESTIGATION.
BE RIGHT BACK!

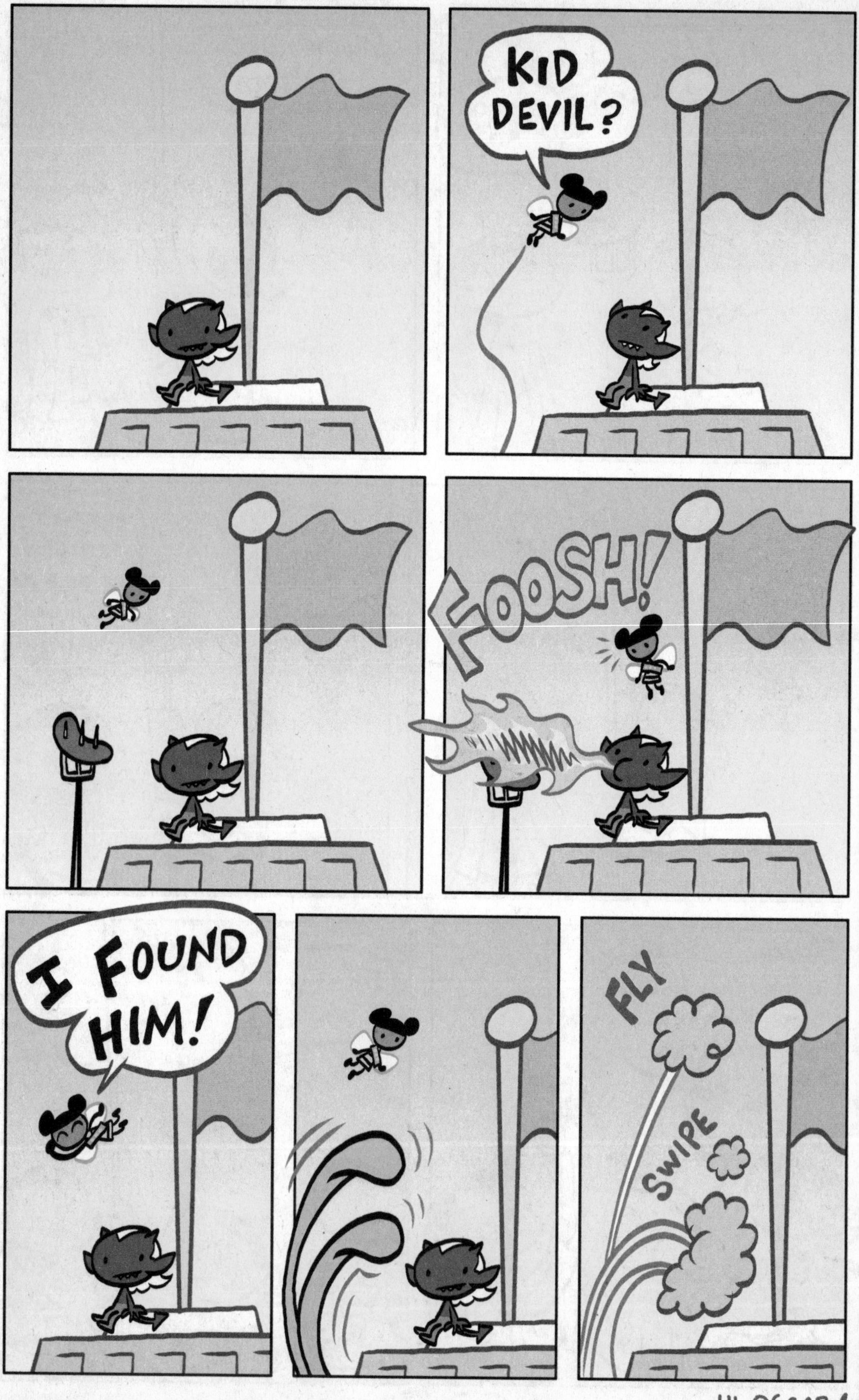
KID DEVIL?
FOOSH!
I FOUND HIM!
FLY
SWIPE

-HI, OSCAR!

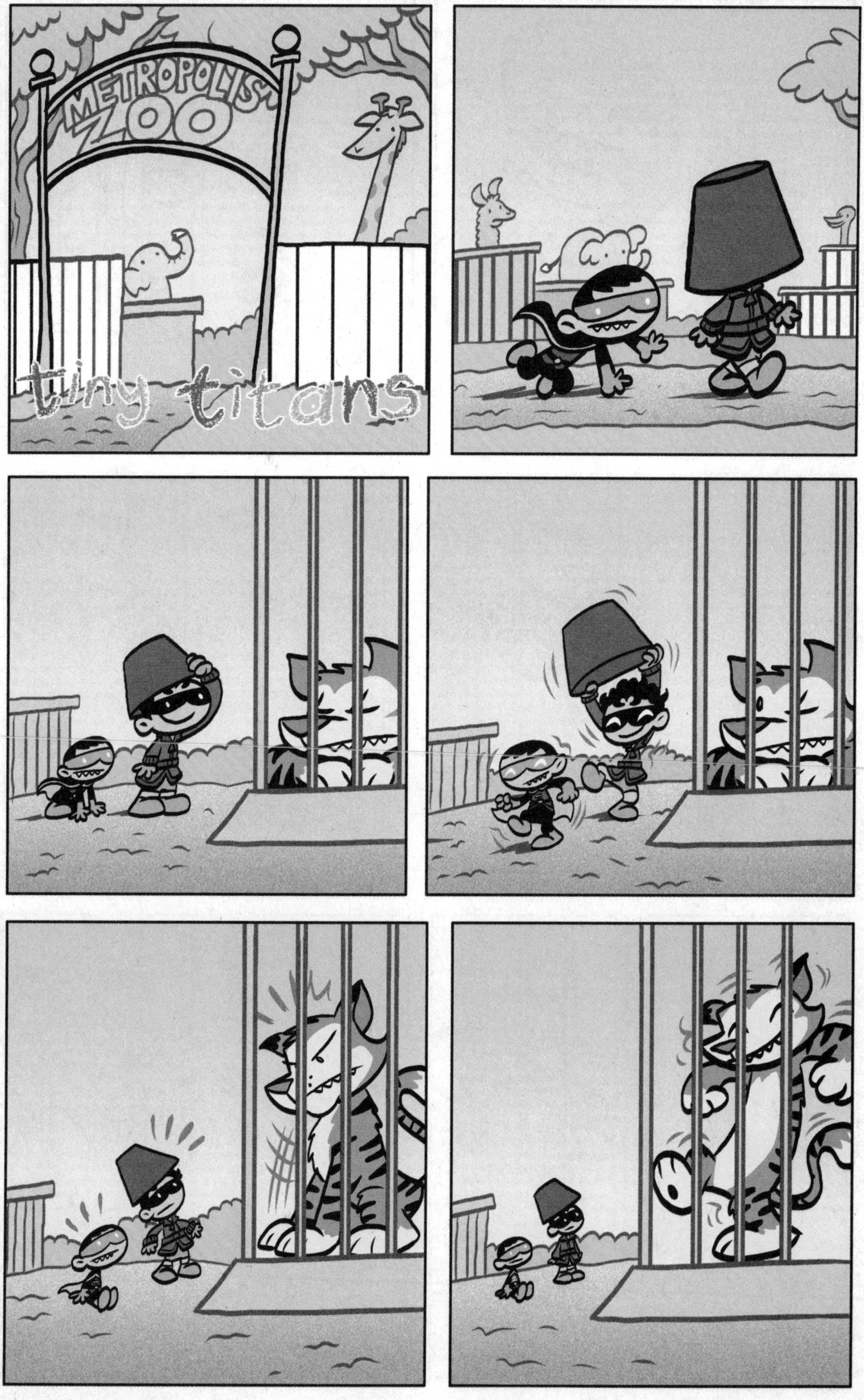
METROPOLIS ZOO
tiny titans

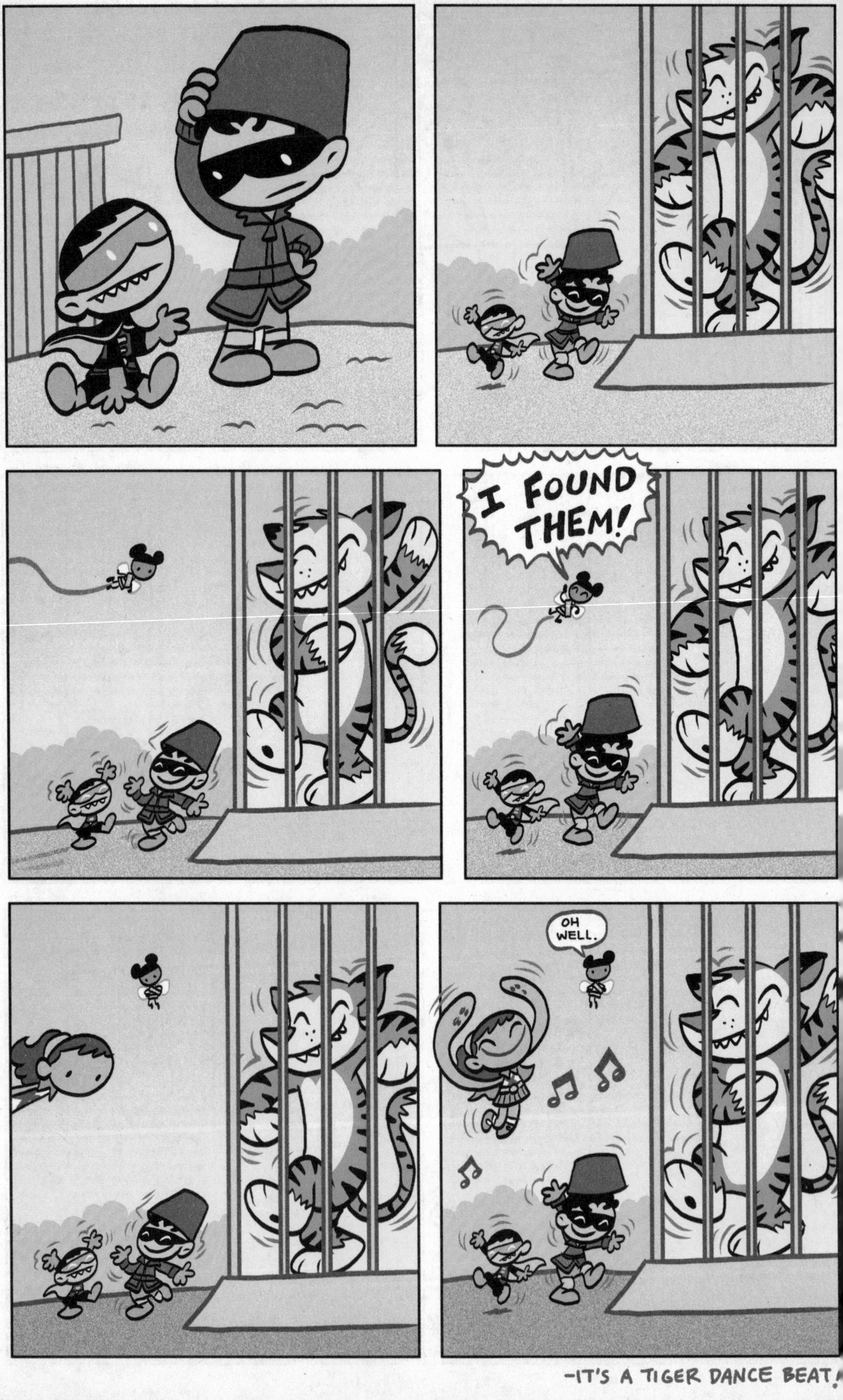
I FOUND THEM!
OH WELL.
-IT'S A TIGER DANCE BEAT!

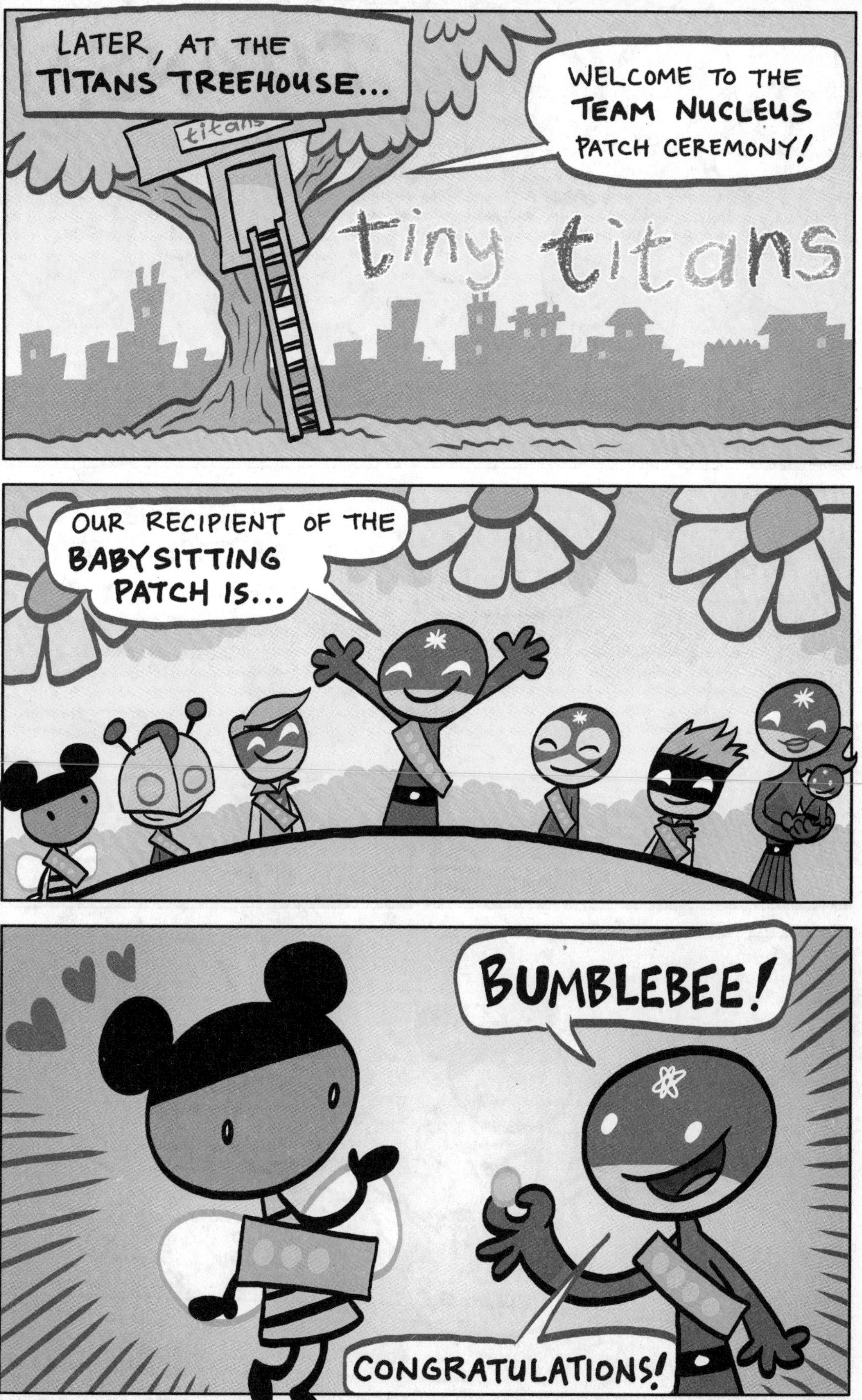

LATER, AT THE TITANS TREEHOUSE...
WELCOME TO THE TEAM NUCLEUS PATCH CEREMONY!
titans
tiny titans
OUR RECIPIENT OF THE BABYSITTING PATCH IS...
BUMBLEBEE!
CONGRATULATIONS!

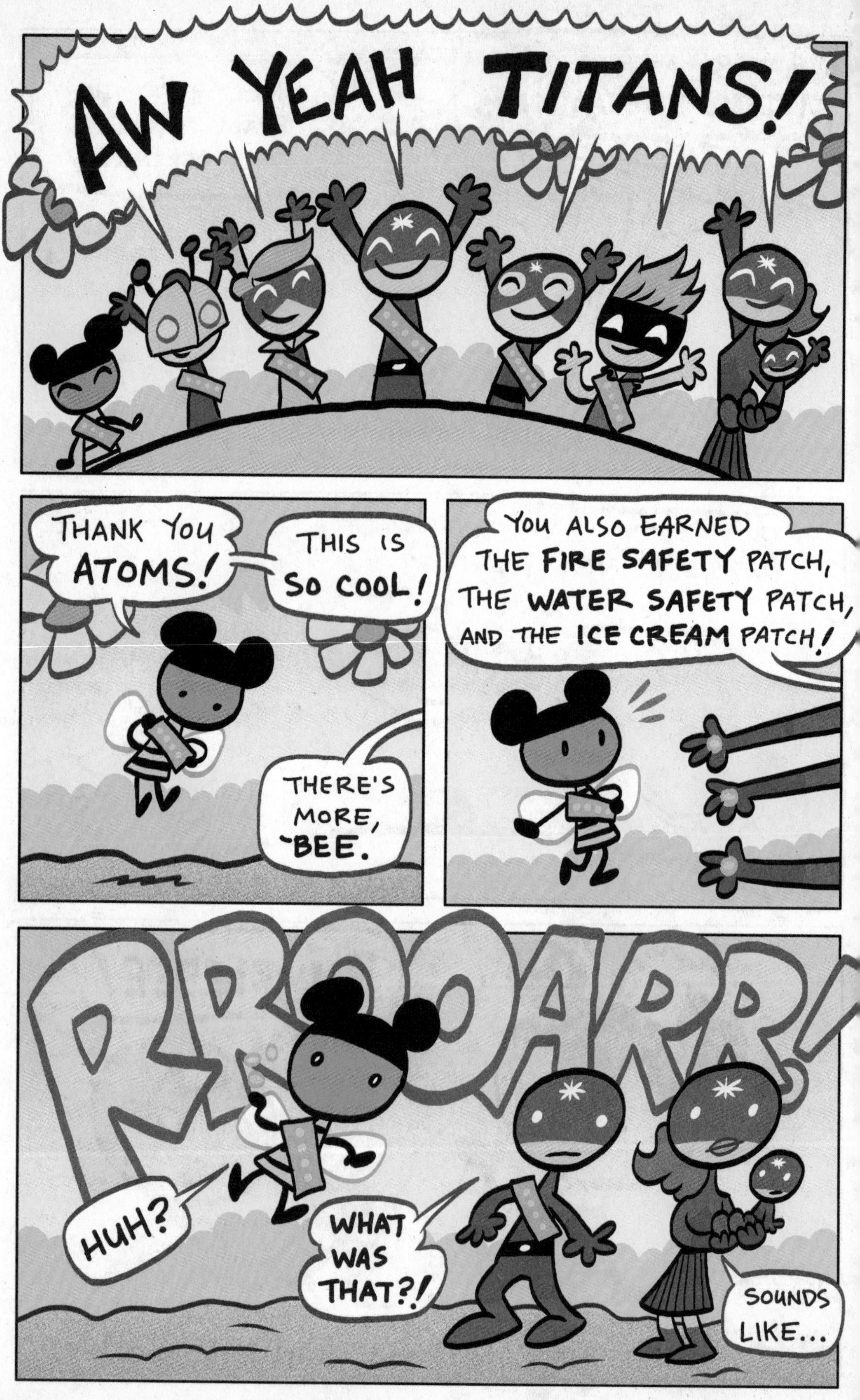
AW YEAH TITANS!
THANK YOU ATOMS!
THIS IS SO COOL!
THERE'S MORE, -BEE.
YOU ALSO EARNED THE FIRE SAFETY PATCH, THE WATER SAFETY PATCH, AND THE ICE CREAM PATCH!
RROOARR!
HUH?
WHAT WAS THAT?!
SOUNDS LIKE...

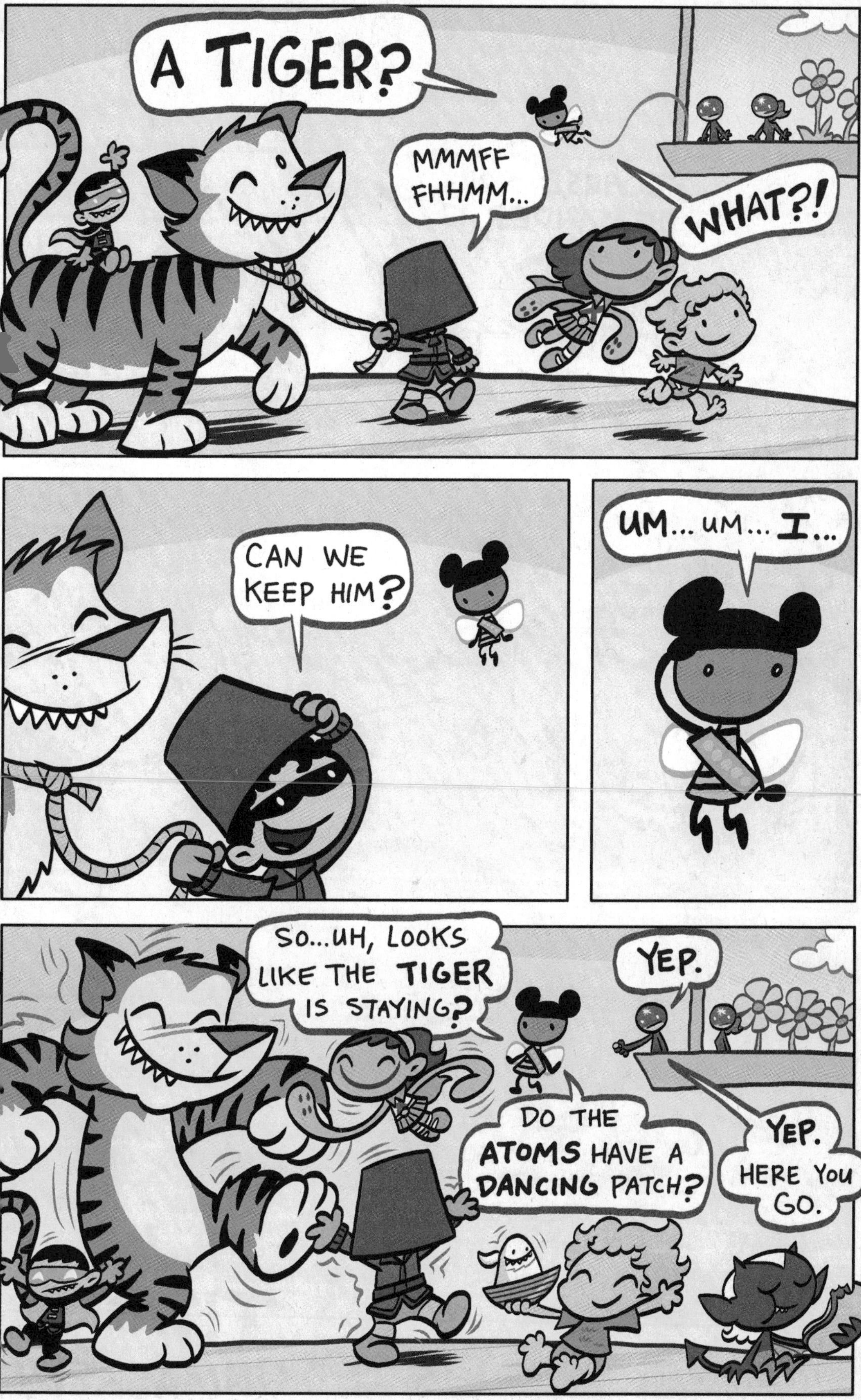
A TIGER?
MMMFF FHHMM...
WHAT?!
CAN WE KEEP HIM?
UM... UM... I...
SO...UH, LOOKS LIKE THE TIGER IS STAYING?
YEP.
DO THE ATOMS HAVE A DANCING PATCH?
YEP. HERE YOU GO.

—WELL EARNED!

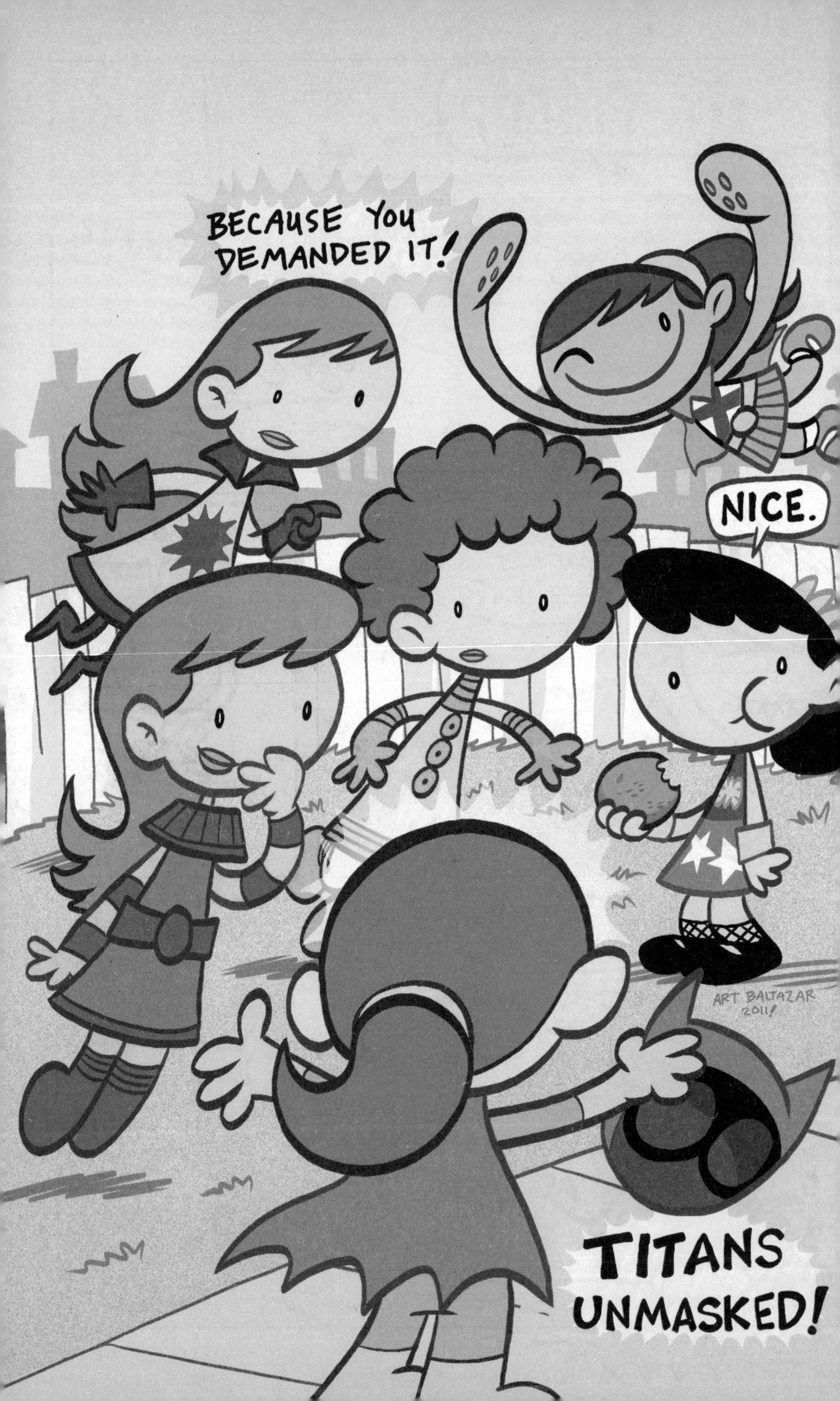
BECAUSE YOU DEMANDED IT!
NICE.
ART BALTAZAR 2011!
TITANS UNMASKED!

—CITRUS!

-WHISPERS

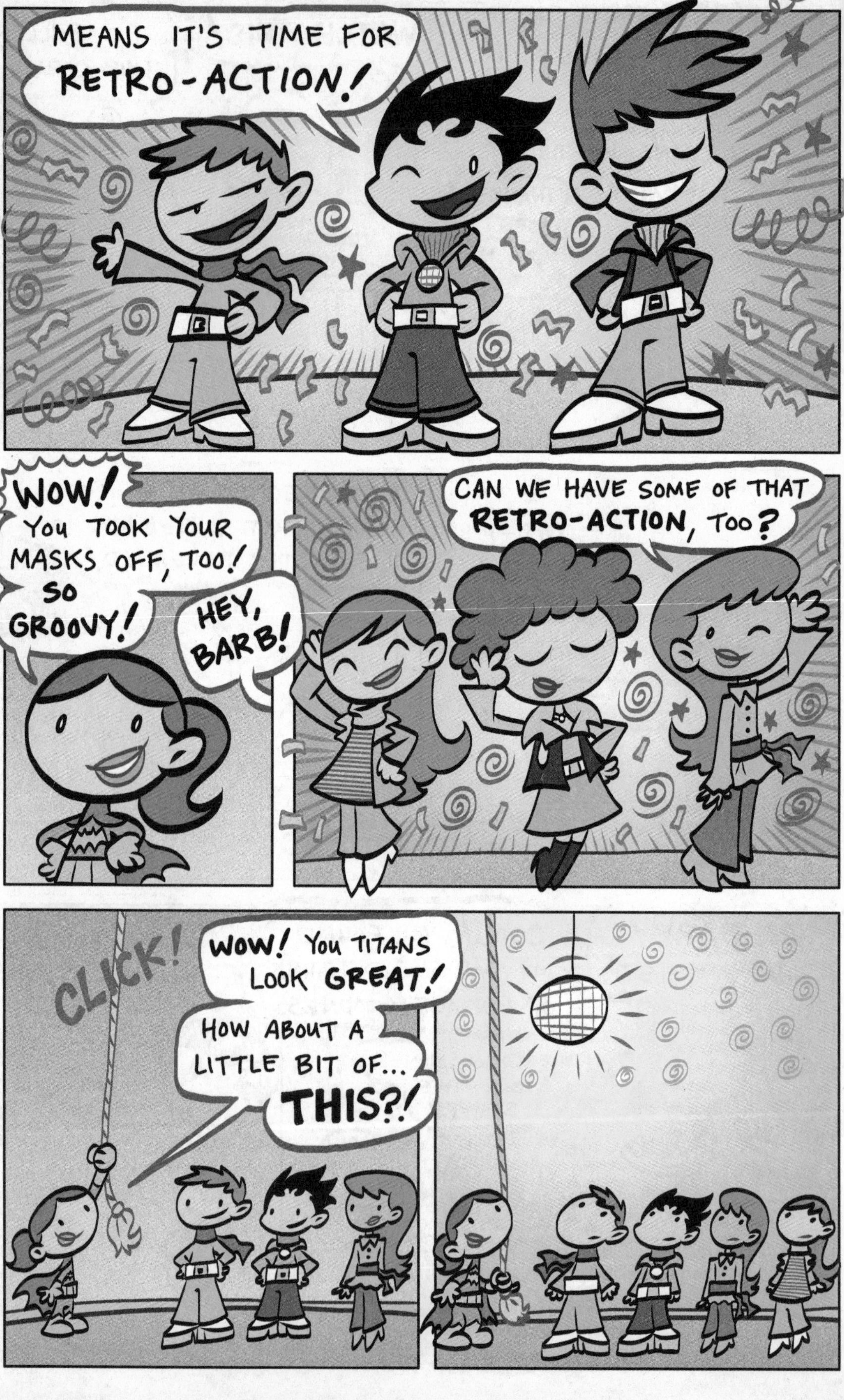

MEANS IT'S TIME FOR RETRO-ACTION!
WOW! YOU TOOK YOUR MASKS OFF, TOO! SO GROOVY!
HEY, BARB!
CAN WE HAVE SOME OF THAT RETRO-ACTION, TOO?
CLICK!
WOW! YOU TITANS LOOK GREAT!
HOW ABOUT A LITTLE BIT OF... THIS?!

-BRIGHTLY SQUEEZED!

-MAGIC LASSO!

—CONTACTS!

-DREAM IT! MAKE IT HAPPEN.

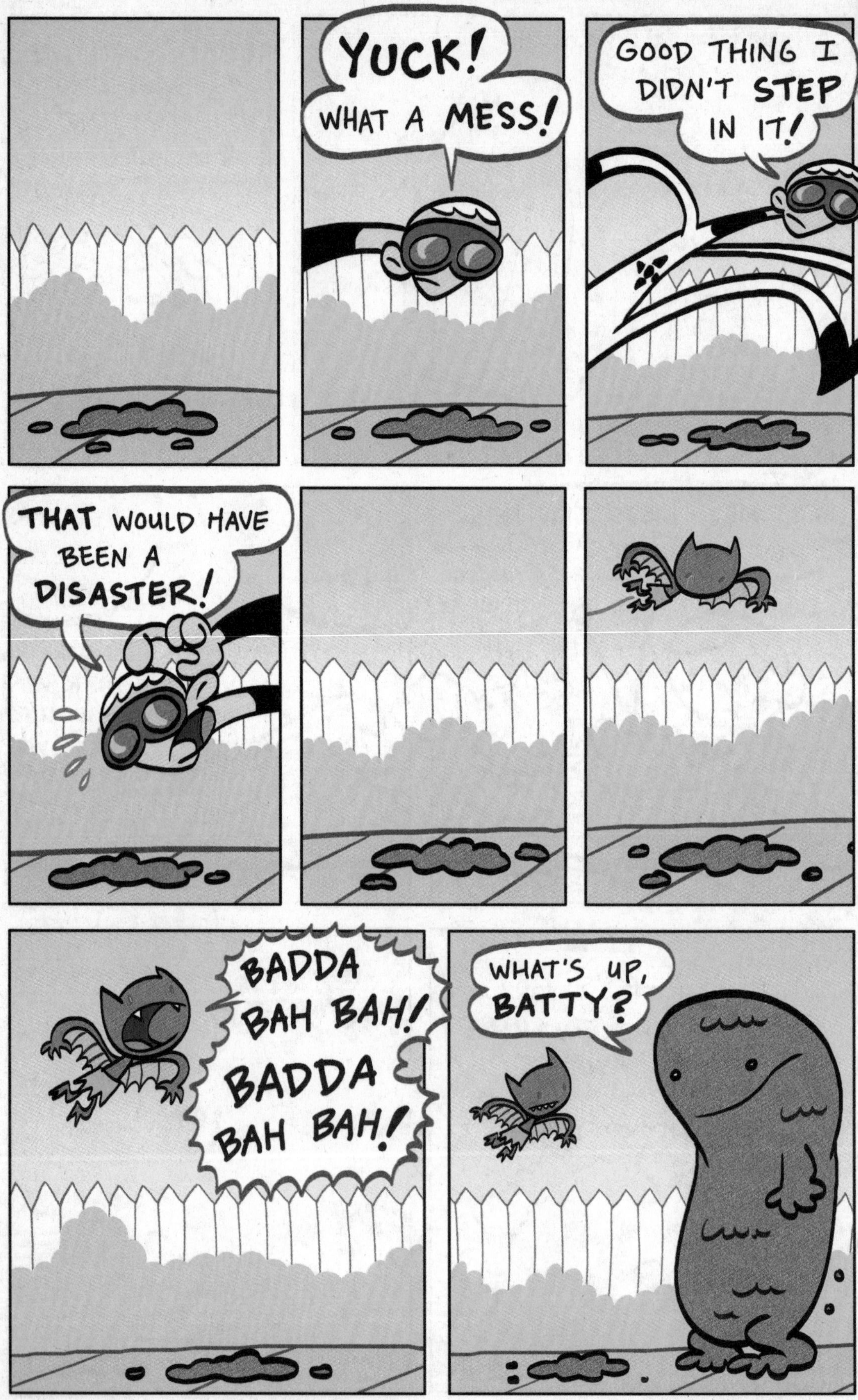

YUCK! WHAT A MESS!
GOOD THING I DIDN'T STEP IN IT!
THAT WOULD HAVE BEEN A DISASTER!
BADDA BAH BAH! BADDA BAH BAH!
WHAT'S UP, BATTY?

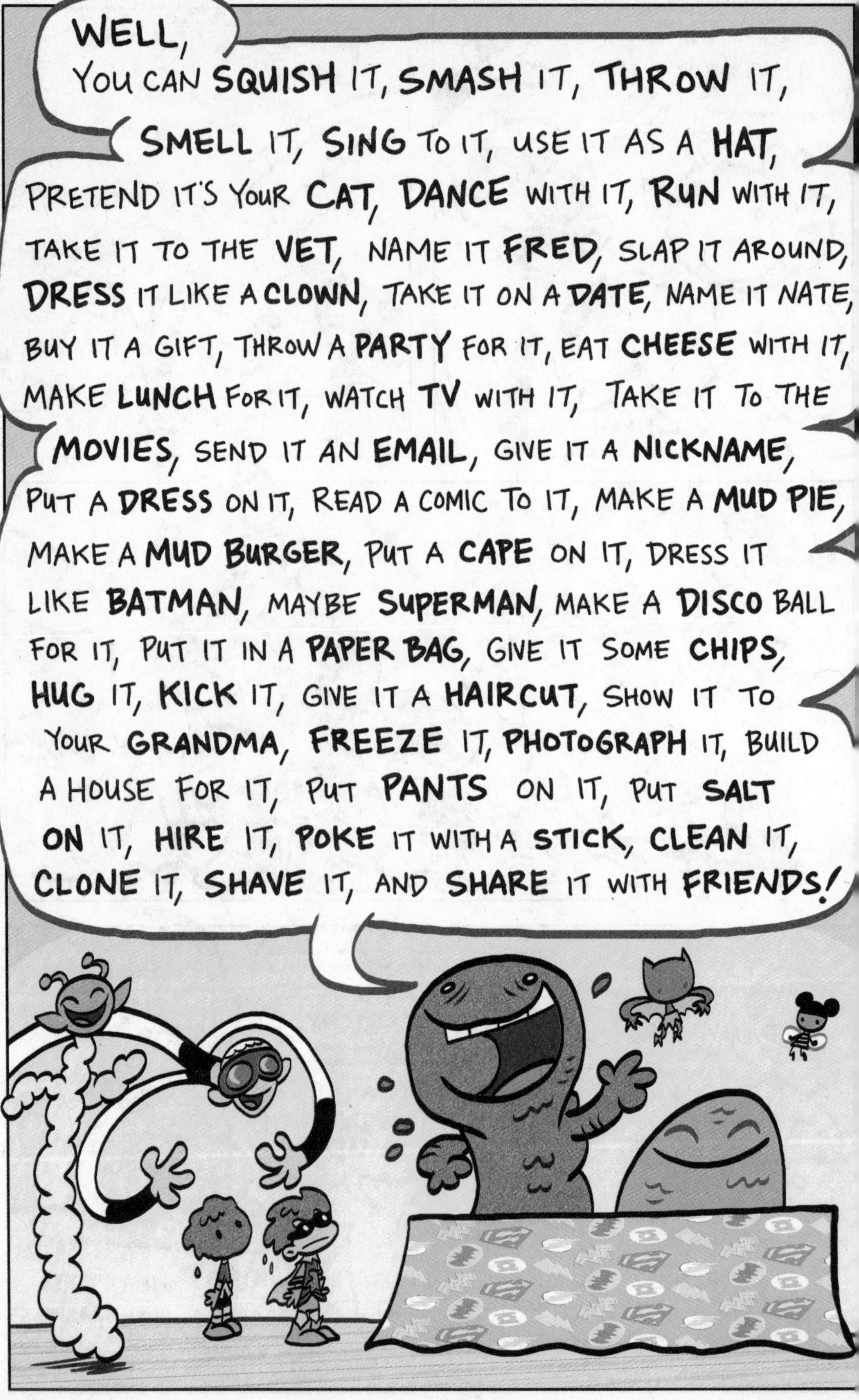
WELL, YOU CAN SQUISH IT, SMASH IT, THROW IT, SMELL IT, SING TO IT, USE IT AS A HAT, PRETEND IT'S YOUR CAT, DANCE WITH IT, RUN WITH IT, TAKE IT TO THE VET, NAME IT FRED, SLAP IT AROUND, DRESS IT LIKE A CLOWN, TAKE IT ON A DATE, NAME IT NATE, BUY IT A GIFT, THROW A PARTY FOR IT, EAT CHEESE WITH IT, MAKE LUNCH FOR IT, WATCH TV WITH IT, TAKE IT TO THE MOVIES, SEND IT AN EMAIL, GIVE IT A NICKNAME, PUT A DRESS ON IT, READ A COMIC TO IT, MAKE A MUD PIE, MAKE A MUD BURGER, PUT A CAPE ON IT, DRESS IT LIKE BATMAN, MAYBE SUPERMAN, MAKE A DISCO BALL FOR IT, PUT IT IN A PAPER BAG, GIVE IT SOME CHIPS, HUG IT, KICK IT, GIVE IT A HAIRCUT, SHOW IT TO YOUR GRANDMA, FREEZE IT, PHOTOGRAPH IT, BUILD A HOUSE FOR IT, PUT PANTS ON IT, PUT SALT ON IT, HIRE IT, POKE IT WITH A STICK, CLEAN IT, CLONE IT, SHAVE IT, AND SHARE IT WITH FRIENDS!

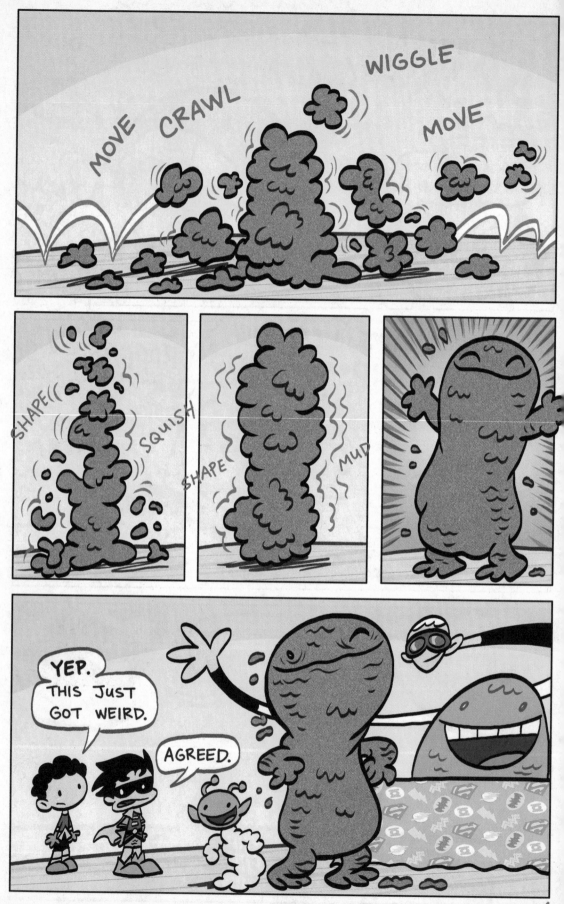

-MOLD IT!

-MYSTERIOUS, TOO.

-RHYMES WITH ORANGE.

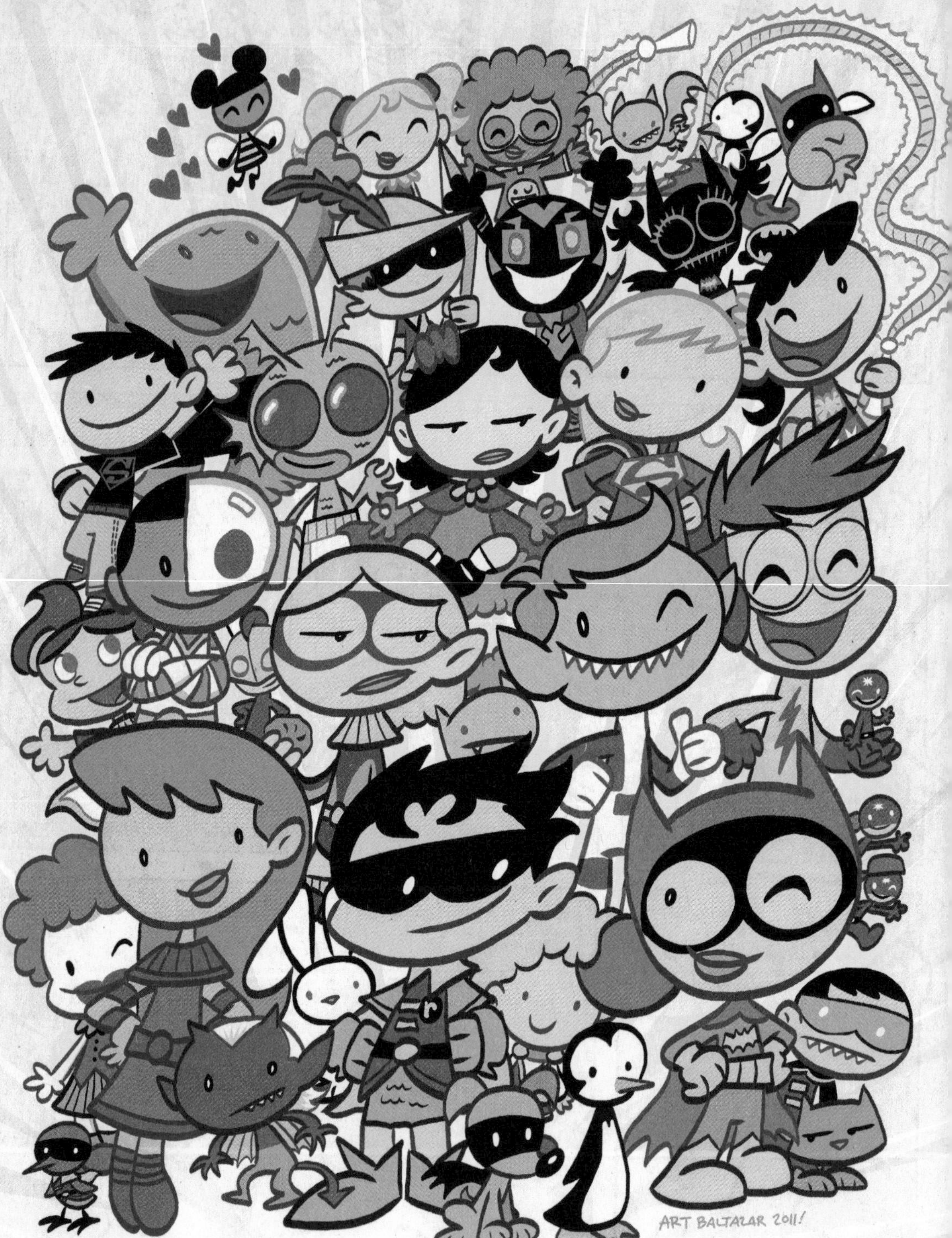
ART BALTAZAR 2011!

tiny titans

-QUESADILLAS!

—NEW WARDROBE IT IS!

—AWARDING!

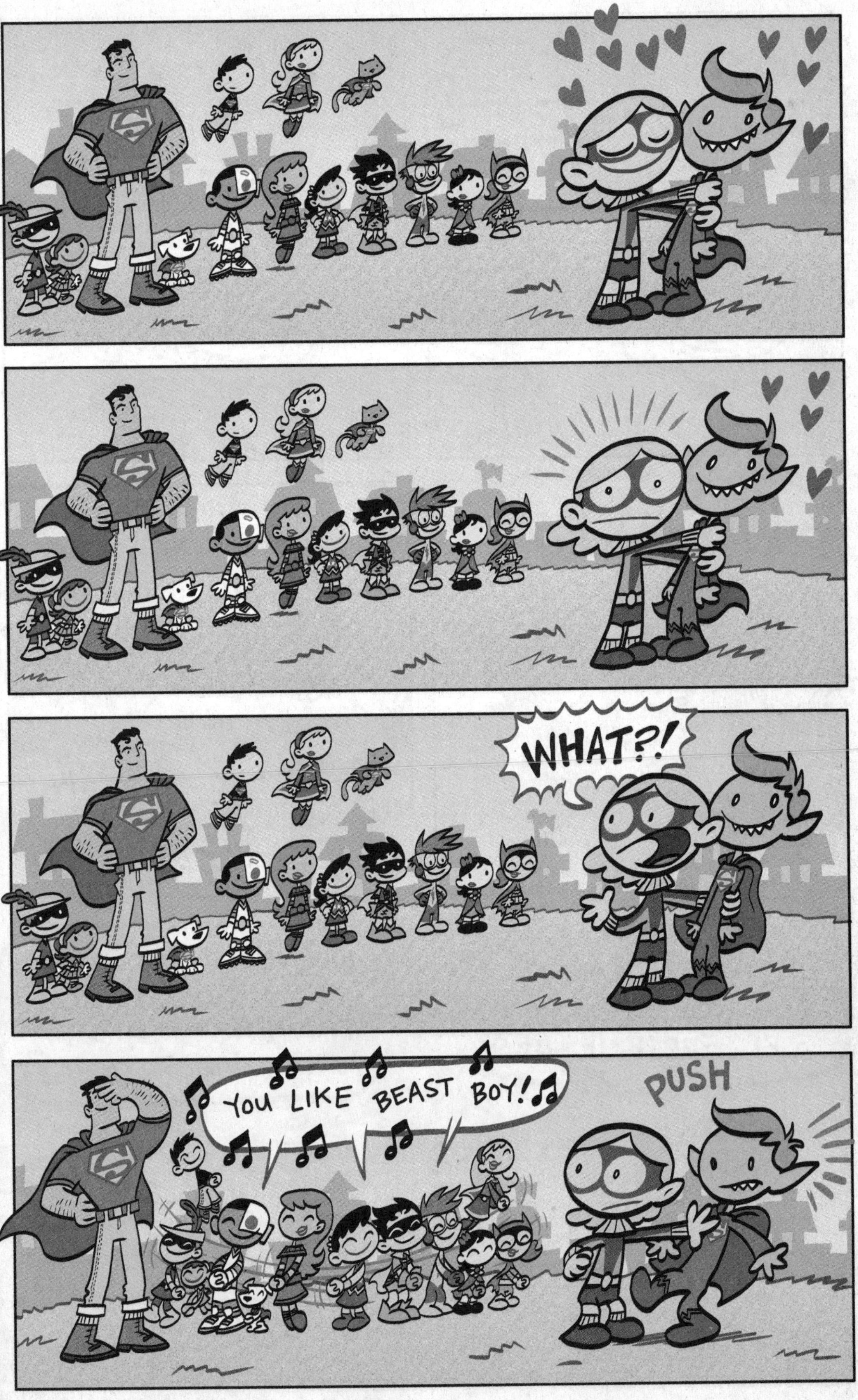
WHAT?!
YOU LIKE BEAST BOY!
PUSH